Basic Instincts

BEYOND THE DARKNESS

THOM COLLINS

ENTWINED PUBLISHING

Beyond the Darkness
ISBN # 978-1-80250-623-5
©Copyright Thom Collins 2025
Cover Art by Kelly Martin ©Copyright October 2025
Interior text design by Entwined Publishing
Published by Evidence, an Entwined Publishing imprint

Published in 2025 by Entwined Publishing, United Kingdom.

Entwined Publishing is a division of Totally Entwined Group Limited.

BEYOND THE DARKNESS

Chapter One

Hate Mail

It was a beautiful Monday morning in late June. Hudson Rhodes decided he would walk all the way from his apartment in the heart of Blyham to the rehearsal studios on the other side of the river. He set off early, full of enthusiasm for the work ahead, stopping only to collect an Americano from the coffee shop on the corner.

Hudson drew the fresh air into his lungs and exhaled with a satisfied sigh. All was good. The first week of any rehearsal was always a stress, getting the words of the play fixed in his head, becoming acquainted with the rest of the cast and crew, but by the time they had quit last Friday, he'd known they were in a strong position.

He'd spent a few additional hours on Saturday working with Julian, a fellow actor who had a small supporting role in *Darkest Blue*. Julian was also understudying Hudson in the lead role of Alan, a morally ambiguous American tourist in 1970s Barcelona. Both from out of town, with little else to do with their weekend, they had put in overtime to work on the nuances of Alan's character and nail the dialogue.

Yes, they were in a great place at the start of the second week. Hudson had insisted on growing his own 1970s style moustache for the play, and even that had filled out in the most impressive way over the last few days. The costume department had initially fitted him with a fake moustache, but he hated to wear it. So much easier and more authentic to sport the real thing.

The city streets were mostly in shade at that time of the morning, until he reached the waterfront. The sun reflected off the surface of the river and held the promise of a golden day to come. Hudson had known very little about Blyham before his arrival the week before. He'd been a New York resident for over a decade, but in the last few years he had spent an increasing amount of time in the UK, working in low-budget movies, TV and theatre. His work had mainly taken him to the major cities — London, Manchester, Birmingham and Edinburgh.

Blyham had come as a pleasant surprise. Much smaller and less metropolitan than he was used to. He'd spent the first few days getting around by Uber and bus, before realising that almost everything was in comfortable walking distance from the apartment. Although his face had started to appear around the city on advertisements for the upcoming play, so far he'd been able to wander without getting recognised too often.

Moving around unnoticed was a trick he'd learnt a long time ago. Invaluable to an actor.

When he reached the Millennium Footbridge, Hudson paused to drink the last of his coffee and enjoy the view. The quayside and waterfront area of the city was quiet and he spent a few moments appreciating the gentle scene. If the second week in the studio were anything like the first, there would not be a lot of time to spend outdoors, or much relaxing. The story and the character he had to play were full-on.

Hudson was ready to embrace it all.

He arrived at the stage door just before nine. It was a full hour before they were due to begin, but he enjoyed the early mornings. Once *Darkest Blue* opened, he would not experience many of those. Evening performances meant not eating until well after eleven and rarely getting to bed before two or three.

Jax, the stage door attendant, greeted him in a buoyant mood when he entered. "How did your weekend go?"

"Very well." Hudson grinned. "I kept a low profile. I attempted to check out a couple of the bars close by, but Saturday night seemed a little wild for me. I was back at the apartment by ten-thirty."

He'd been amazed to discover that the apartment building overlooked a sex club called The Viaduct. He'd amused himself for twenty minutes or so, watching all the guys lining up to go in while he'd enjoyed a nightcap on his balcony. Blyham might be a small city, but it seemed to have plenty going on.

Jax grimaced. "If I'm not working, I stay well clear on Saturdays. This place doesn't just get wild, it goes mental. Too much for me these days." She rummaged beneath the desk and produced a pile of mail, secured together with an elastic band. "Fan mail, I assume. It arrived over the weekend."

"For me? Really. I'm surprised anyone knows I'm here." Hudson considered himself to be a working actor. He had appeared in a handful of high-profile projects, together with some movies that had attained cult status, but he was not a major star. Fan mail made him uncomfortable, especially as it was not always welcome.

"Autograph collectors, I expect," Jax said. "There are a few of them locally who write to everyone who appears here. You're also likely to get some autograph dealers turning up after the show with a pile of glossy photos for you to sign. eBay professionals."

Hudson chuckled. "I'm familiar with the type." He shoved the bundle under his arm. "Is anyone else here yet?"

"You're the first." Jax released the security door and handed him a visitor pass.

Blyham Concert Hall was a relatively modern building filled with state-of-the-art equipment and spaces. From the outside, it was an impressive site, all floor to ceiling, mirrored windows. The interiors were bright, cool and uncluttered. The play was actually being staged in the more traditional Empire Theatre on the other side of the river, but as there was already a show running there, the production had hired rooms here for the first three weeks of rehearsal.

Hudson made his way to the large, airy room on the first floor, which looked across the river and the buildings beyond. This really was a sweet little city. Once the play had opened and he had more time for himself, he looked forward to exploring further and discovering all it had to offer. There was even a castle a little way down the river that he couldn't wait to check out.

Last week, the room had been set with a large centre table for the cast and crew to read around. Most of that had been cleared over the weekend, creating a wide, open floor space ready for week two's more practical rehearsals. He got a glass of water and sat down to look over his mail.

He opened the largest envelope first.

The hairs on the back of his neck prickled immediately.

A glossy eight-by-ten photo slid onto the table. It was a shot from a low-budget horror movie he had made in his early twenties, almost twenty years ago. *Red Hills Massacre*. The scene shown had not even made it into the finished film, having been considered too graphic by the ratings board of the time. Even so, it was an image that provoked uncomfortable memories for him.

He was dressed in nothing but a pair of once-pristine tighty-whiteys. His chest and neck were fitted with elaborate make-up effects to represent brutal injuries. His youthful body was splayed at an unnatural angle, but the camera focused on his bloodied crotch area. With his thighs splayed, it was a gory display of eroticism and death. In the movie, his character was murdered after a prolonged chase by a madman in a mask.

All in his underpants.

Hudson shook out the envelope to see what else was in there. A single note dropped out.

How I like to picture you.

That was it. No request for him to sign the photo or any address to return it to.

Shit. He was no stranger to weird mail, and this rang a very familiar alarm bell.

He checked the envelope again. Like the note inside, the address had been printed. The postmark was from Blyham itself. As he looked at the next item of mail, cold fingers of dread skittered down his spine. The envelope was different, but the print was exactly the same. Inside was another photograph. Another image from *Red Hills Massacre*. He was in his tight white underpants again, only this time he wasn't dead. It showed his character walking through his house, unaware of the killer right behind, the grisly axe raised to strike. The killer in the movie was nicknamed Baby Face on account of the creepy baby mask he wore. A grinning face with a single tooth. This time the message with the photo read *Dead man walking*, followed by a smiling emoji.

Who the hell would waste their time bothering to send him these? Hudson had a sneaky suspicion but didn't want to risk manifesting it by even acknowledging the idea.

There were two more similar photos and messages — *Soon you die* and *Pretty boy dead* — then a couple of seemingly genuine letters from people saying they couldn't wait to see him in the show. By the time he got to them, he was so unsettled he couldn't take in what the writers were saying.

The spell was broken by voices in the corridor. The door opened and the director and the producer arrived together, full of new-week enthusiasm. Andie Shapiro was one of the most acclaimed theatre directors in recent years, with smash-hit shows in London and New York. A large black woman in her mid-fifties, she had a personal style ran to colourful silk blouses and masses of jewellery.

"Hey, an actor who can get out of bed on a morning," she declared in a booming voice as she caught sight of Hudson. "I like it. This is going to be a great week. I can feel it already."

Even the producer, Rav Millard, was smiling. Rav was fifty-five, overweight and, from Hudson's impression of him so far, permanently stressed. "Morning, Hudson. Good to see you so keen."

Andie enveloped Hudson in a wide hug and breathed air kisses on his cheeks. "I hope you got plenty of rest over the weekend. You're going to need all your energy." As she stood back, she spotted the spread of photos on the table. "What's all this?" The note of caution in her voice was unmistakable.

"I just collected them from the stage door," he explained, leafing through the pictures. "Grim, aren't they? I hate that fucking movie."

Rav gathered up the photos and envelopes. "Who gave them to you?" He stacked them in an untidy heap and shoved them under his arm.

"I told you. I just collected them from the stage door." He caught the look that passed between Rav and Andie.

"We've got people to handle your fan mail," Rav said. "You don't need to waste your time on nonsense like this. Just pre-sign a stack of promos and we'll mail them out on your behalf." He looked away from Hudson, avoiding his eyes.

"They're not asking for autographs. Well, apart from a couple. The rest are just weird." Now Andie was avoiding his gaze, seemingly transfixed by something important on her phone. The sense of unease that had been with him since he'd opened the mail continued to grow. "Have there been more of these?" Today was the first time he'd been handed his mail at the stage door. For the whole of the first week there had been nothing. "Have there?"

Andie gave him a reassuring smile. "It's nothing. A needless distraction, that's all."

He stiffened. "It's a little more than that, I'd say. Someone has gone to the trouble of getting those shots printed, those particular shots, and posted them here with their creepy messages. *Pretty boy dead.* How many more of these has there been?"

Another loaded glance between the director and the producer.

"A few," Rav said.

"But it's nothing," Andie said. "Just some sad case getting a cheap thrill."

His head was spinning. "Are they all like this?"

The silence was palpable.

"Pretty much," Andie admitted after a long pause.

Hudson put his figures to his temples, trying to contain his vexing thoughts. "You've been keeping it from me."

"It's for the best," Rav said. "Look how unsettled it's made you today. It's just some rando trying to freak you out. Not worth worrying about."

He laughed incredulously. He wanted to be angry. He wanted to swear and rage at this pair for what they'd taken upon themselves to do. "You do know what happened to me before? I've had experience of this shit. I've had to take out court orders over stuff like this."

"I'm sure this is not that serious," Andie said.

"The fucking post marks are right from this city. Whoever sent those is nearby."

"A keyboard warrior," Rav said brightly. "You know what they're like."

"We all do," Andie added.

"They tend to stick to online trolling. Not posting photographs of me covered in blood in just my underwear."

14

"We've already got a security team looking at this." Andie's voice was calm and level. "It's a precaution. I'm sure there's nothing to worry about, and we won't let anything happen to you. Rav will pass on this latest delivery, and they'll see what they can do with it. Someone is trying to unsettle you. To throw you off your game. Don't allow that to happen."

"Let us take care of this," Rav said, seeming to grow in confidence. "You need to focus on what you've got to do and let me worry about whatever dipshit is sending this stuff. We'll find them and warn them off."

"He's right," Andie said. "You were brilliant last week and you're going to blow people's minds when this play opens. Don't let a minor distraction get in the way of that. All celebrities get sent shit like this — you know that. It's nothing. Some sad little reject trying to make themselves feel important. That can only happen if you allow it."

Hudson took a long slow breath. He knew what they were up to. They were more concerned with their own agenda of getting the play on than they were about him, but beneath it all, he agreed with them. He'd flown all this way because he wanted this role. The play was launching with a four-week run in Blyham, but all indications were that it would open in the West End next year if it went down well here. He couldn't lose sight of that goal.

"You shouldn't have kept this from me," he said. "I want to know if there are any further developments. If they find who is sending them, or if the content gets worse."

"For sure," Rav said. He waved the pile of mail. "I'll get on it now."

Andie gave a wide smile. "Excellent. Now, let's not waste any more time, eh?" She reached over and ran her fingers across Hudson's face. "The 'tache is fabulous, by the way. It looks so sexy on you."

She hefted her enormous handbag onto the table and began pulling out scripts, pens, and a packet of cigarettes.

Hudson couldn't stay mad, despite himself. It was time to focus. Even still, it would be a while before he could shake the sense of unease those images and messages had aroused.

Chapter Two

Well Packaged Bad News

"I can't believe she said that."

"Yep." Hudson nodded. "Apparently my moustache is more important than my well-being."

Julian King chuckled. "I'm glad I only have to wear the fake one. It does look great on you, though. You should take the compliment."

In the last week, Hudson and Julian had become good friends. The closest he'd come to anyone in the production so far. Julian was playing the role of an interfering tourist, while also understudying Hudson in the lead part. He was around six or seven years younger than Hudson, and British, but they'd been surprised to discover they had so much in common, bonding over their mutual appreciation of movies, music and books, as well as their understanding of the play.

Rehearsals had gone on until well after six. Afterwards, Hudson and Julian had crossed the river to The Blue Pearl, a cool bar they had discovered the week before that specialised in good food and live entertainment. They were currently in between sets of a young singer and guitarist, who played a handful of his own songs.

Rav had taken away the photos that had come in the mail, so Hudson had to show Julian examples from the movie on his phone.

"You look so young," Julian said, checking out the gallery of stills from *Red Hills Massacre*.

"Twenty-one, maybe twenty-two. I don't remember exactly when we shot it. I had to go back for reshoots after the main production wrapped because my original death scene was too violent and intense."

"I don't think I've even seen it. I'm not big on horror films. My God, that mask is creepy as hell," he said as he swiped to an image of the killer.

"You're not missing much with this one. I wish I'd never done the fucking thing. I was a last-minute replacement for someone who dropped out, the lucky bastard. That film has brought me nothing but bad luck."

"How come?"

He groaned. "Long, long story. Let's not go into it now. I need to keep my head straight for the play."

"You looked good, though," Julian said, handing back the phone. "You still do, but you were a real hottie in those days. If I had pics of me looking so good in my undies, I'd be posting them everywhere. I'd probably use them as my profile picture now."

Hudson grimaced. "I attracted all the wrong kinds of attention for it." The fact that some loser was still fixated on the image of him from twenty years ago proved that nothing much had changed. Sure, he had looked great at the time, but it was a simple fact of having to. There'd been no such thing as a normal body type in the industry when he started. If young actors had wanted to secure any type of work, they'd needed a certain look—ripped abs, bulging biceps and huge pecs. Hudson had achieved that physique with extreme diets, obsession, exercise regimes and steroids. Totally unhealthy.

He still worked out and ate reasonably well now, but it was all about maintaining good health rather than trying to look hot.

The Blue Pearl seemed busy for a Monday evening. He guessed that the live music was a big draw. He checked out the posters that were dotted about the place and noted they had two or three different acts on each night, catering to all genres, even more so at the weekend. When the play opened, he wouldn't have a lot of time to socialise, but he could already see himself enjoying his Sunday afternoons off in this place.

"How are things with Manuella?" he asked.

Julian gave a sheepish grin. Manuella, a stunning Spanish model, was making her theatre debut in *Darkest Blue*. She was bright and intelligent, but deeply insecure about her performance. It had been obvious from the moment they had met in rehearsals last week that Manuella and Julian couldn't keep their eyes off each other. "She's going to call me later, so we can go over a scene together."

"That's progress." Hudson found it kind of sweet that they had not torn each other's clothes off at the first opportunity and appeared to be enjoying some kind of old-fashioned courtship. He hoped it worked out for them.

Julian made a move to go to the bathroom. "I'll get us another drink on my way back, then I'll get going. I want to keep a clear head for later."

The bar had filled up around them and Hudson noticed that a lot of the tables outside were also occupied. It was a beautiful evening, and the small outdoor terrace was perfectly placed to catch the late sun. The young singer had returned to the stage and was arranging his equipment for his next set.

Hudson's eyes were drawn to an exceptionally handsome man at the far end of the bar. He stood with an older man, who had his back to Hudson, but he had noticed Hudson too. The man glanced over his companion's shoulder to look at him more than once.

Hello, good-looking.

Hudson had been so focused on preparing for the play in recent weeks that he had barely looked twice at any hot guy. He hadn't even used any hook-up apps to check out the local guys. But there was no ignoring this knockout.

He was tall, a good few inches taller than himself, he would guess, with short, very dark hair and chiselled cheekbones. There was dark stubble on his lean jaw. His looks were almost brooding, until the man he was with said something which caused him to break into the most disarming smile.

Fuck me! He's stunning.

He wore light suit trousers and an open-necked white shirt. Strong pecs pressed against the shirt front, and the outline of his nipples was visible.

Hudson felt a stirring inside his pants. He didn't want to stare in a creepy way—he knew how unwelcome that could be—but this guy was like a magnet for his eyes. *How old is he?* Younger than Hudson, but not by much. Mid to late thirties. There was definite maturity in those fine good looks, but a playful sense of youth in that smile and his twinkling eyes. There was a hint of widow's peak on his hairline that also suggested he was more man than boy.

Hudson took a swig of beer and forced himself to watch the stage, realising he was getting hot around the neck and throat. This guy was having a big impact on him.

He was about to get out his phone and log into Grindr to see if this hottie was also online when Julian returned with two fresh bottles of beer. They sat quietly and watched the singer for a while. He performed a set of acoustic rock and indie songs. Hudson realised he'd spent enough time in the UK in recent years to recognise a lot of the songs.

"He's great," he said.

Julian agreed. "They've got another guy on towards the end of the week, Friday I think, who could be worth a look if you fancy it?"

"Sounds good. I really like this place."

At the end of the next song, Julian excused himself. "Got to go. I want to get back to the hotel before Manuella calls."

They hugged goodbye and Julian set off. Hudson decided he'd finish his drink and call it a night too. He didn't want a heavy head for the rehearsals tomorrow. They were planning to run through the first act in its entirety and he wanted to be good. When the singer completed his set, Hudson gave him a warm applause and knocked off his beer. It was after eight. He should be back at the apartment well before nine. He would relax for a while on the balcony then get an early night.

The handsome man was still at the end of the bar. Their eyes locked once more as Hudson stood. Hudson gave him a friendly smile of acknowledgement and his cock stirred as he walked out of the door. Maybe another time, when he had less on his mind.

The sun was hidden behind the high buildings when he stepped out, but it was still a fine and clement evening. He decided to take the long way back. He would go down to the river and follow the waterfront for a while, before heading up into the city.

"Excuse me," a voice called from behind. "Mr Rhodes."

He turned, stunned to find the hot guy from the bar following him. The warm sensation returned to Hudson's neck, climbing over his face. His balls tightened.

As the man approached, the dazzling smile was at full voltage. He was even more attractive than he had appeared from a distance.

And he already knew who Hudson was.

"Hi," he said, coming closer. Was that a flush of red in his cheeks and neck? "Sorry to bother you. I didn't like to disturb you earlier, I just wanted to say hello." He had a strong accent that Hudson had come to recognise as being unique to this city. He was familiar with Geordie, and this was similar, but softer, sexier.

Hudson returned the smile, full on. This guy was not like the typical fans who approached him for selfies. On the whole, he mostly got recognised for a handful of cheesy romcoms he'd made in his late twenties and early thirties, and it was often women who flagged him down.

Through the open neck of the man's shirt, he caught a teasing glimpse of dark chest hair. Hudson's dick swelled to a semi state.

"Luke Kamal," the man said, thrusting his hand forward.

Hudson took it welcomingly, noting the firm, dry grip. "Hi, Luke. I guess you know who I am."

Luke's dark eyes focused directly on him, and it was quite disarming. Hudson had worked with some world-famous actors and heartthrobs and very few of them possessed the raw magnetism of this stranger.

"You're quite a big deal around here. Everyone is excited about the play launching in Blyham."

Luke was an apparent flatterer, but he was so good-looking Hudson took his comment as a compliment rather than pure bullshit. "You're coming to see the show then?"

That smile again, then Luke broke eye contact, seemingly shy. It was quite endearing. "You could say that. Actually, I'll be there tomorrow. That's why I wanted to say hello when I spotted you. It seemed rude not to."

For a second, Hudson wondered if he was so hypnotised by this hot man that he'd misheard what he'd said. *And damn, he smells great too.* "Oh, we don't actually open for a couple more weeks. The first preview is early next month, I think."

"I'll be there for that too, but I'll be there tomorrow for the rehearsals." The blank expression on Hudson's face seemed to confuse him too. He continued. "Luke Kamal, from *The Blyham Chronicle*. I'm the arts and culture editor. Well, editor is putting it grandly, but I cover all the major arts, music and theatre events for the paper. We're going to run a major feature on *Darkest Blue* over the next few weeks — that's why I'm sitting in on rehearsals for a few days."

Again, Luke's words were not computing with Hudson. "Wait, you're a journalist...? You're going to watch us put the show together?"

The smile wavered then disappeared. "It's been arranged for weeks. I thought you knew."

Hudson withdrew into himself, trying to make sense of what he'd heard. *What the actual fuck?* How the hell were they supposed to dig deep into themselves, to make themselves vulnerable in search of the characters and stories, with a reporter watching and taking note of every fuck-up, every misstep?

"That can't be right," he managed. "You've got it wrong."

Luke fumbled in his trousers, pulled out a leather wallet and produced his press card. "It's all legit. I'm due there at ten tomorrow and then in and out all the way to opening night."

"Not if I have anything to do with it," Hudson muttered.

"I'm sorry. I thought they would have told you. Hasn't it been cleared with the cast?"

"No, it fucking well hasn't." Hudson's lust for Luke was on the verge of turning into anger. Not just at him but at Rav and Andie and this whole damn shit-show of a production. "This is outrageous," he said through gritted teeth.

Luke's brow shot up in alarm. "Look, Hudson, Mr Rhodes. I don't think I've explained myself very well. This isn't some undercover exposé. I'm not coming to write a hatchet piece on the play. I want *Darkest Blue* to succeed. We all do. That's why I'll be there. To give the show some great publicity and get the word out. This is a big deal for Blyham. To have a major new production try out here with an international star, ahead of a sure-fire West End transfer. It's massive for our region. We only want the best."

The calming words and soft tone had zero effect on Hudson. "That all sounds peachy, and you flatter me, Mr Kamal." Sarcasm dripped from every word. "But you're a journalist and I've heard this kind of smooth bullshit a million times before. And guess what, it never turned out well. I'm not about to get a poisoned pen stuck in my ribs again."

"I can assure you —"

"Save it," Hudson snapped. "I'm not interested. I don't know what that asshole Rav has promised you, but if I have anything to do with it, it won't be happening. You can write all you want after opening night, but you won't be sitting in on any of my rehearsals."

Luke straightened, holding out his chest, his jaw set firm. "It's already been agreed. I'll be there tomorrow whether you like it or not. For the sake of everyone — for the sake of the show — it would be much easier if we could all see eye to eye on this."

Hudson turned and hurried away without another word, his anger intensifying with each incensed step. First the fucking hate mail, now this good-looking bastard journo.

He had a growing feeling that this play was cursed from the start.

Chapter Three

A History of Stalking

After a restless night in which he failed to get any benefit from going to bed early, Hudson was in no better mood about the current situation. He got up at six and went for a workout in a nearby gym. Sweating it out with weights and thirty minutes running full-out on the treadmill didn't help much either. He showered and dressed and, after struggling to eat breakfast, he fired off a text to Rav and Andie telling them he wanted to see them at the studio early, before anyone else arrived.

"Most of all the fucking reporter," he muttered to himself.

As he'd tossed about during the night, he'd replayed the conversation with Luke Kamal over and over. Hudson wasn't proud of the way he'd handled it, losing his temper and storming off in a rage, but he'd been ill equipped to deal with it any other way at the time. The news had floored him. It wasn't Luke's fault they were in that situation. He probably thought he was doing Hudson a favour by speaking to him first.

Luke was just doing his job. *Ha*. How many shitty journalists had said that to him over the years? They were only ever doing their jobs, regardless of who they hurt, burned or stomped into the dust in the process. Hudson's knuckles were white as he gripped his coffee cup.

Eventually, he gave up on breakfast, loaded the dishwasher and left the apartment.

It was another glorious morning, but he was in no mood to appreciate it as he walked down to the waterfront and over the bridge. Even the tranquil beauty of the river failed to calm him.

"This is even earlier than yesterday," Jax said when he arrived. "You do know there'll be no one to let you in if you get here before eight, right?"

"I don't plan to make a habit of it." His smile and tone of voice were forced. Hardly one of his better performances. "Any mail today?"

Jax ducked to look beneath the counter. He silently prayed that she would come up empty-handed.

"You must have quite a fanbase," she said, handing him a bundle. "There's even more than yesterday. Those posters of you all over town must be doing the trick."

"Must be," he commented without enthusiasm. One glance at the letter on top and a cloud of resignation came over him. He recognised the printed label and had no doubts about what was inside. "I don't suppose Rav and Andie are here yet?"

Jax shook her head and checked her watch. "Should they be?"

"Yep. Tell them I'm in the rehearsal room and want to see them right away."

He got himself a drink and sat at the table, before opening the first letter. It was another photo like before, a different still of him in his underwear from *Red Hills Massacre*. Another image from his unused, ultra-gory death scene. He wondered how the hell this stuff had even made it into the public domain. The scenes had been cut from the film due to their graphic content, but they were all over the internet. These days the deleted footage was even on YouTube. If the studio hadn't wanted it released, how come it was so freely available?

And why was it such a magnet for weirdos? When *Red Hills Massacre* fans wrote to him or arrived at stage doors with their memorabilia to be signed, they were all more interested in the deleted footage than what was actually in the movie. Hudson couldn't claim to have a preference for either version. The re-shot murder scene was just as disturbing, possibly even worse, as it left more to the viewers' imagination.

And what an imagination some of them had.

The latest message read *Hudson Rhodes Massacre*.

"How bloody original," he muttered, stuffing it all back into the envelope.

He decided not to open any of the other letters. If there was information to be gained about who was sending these, he would only contaminate the evidence.

Hudson already had a suspicion.

Rav and Andie arrived a little before nine.

"Morning, handsome." Andie bustled in like nothing was wrong. She had her huge handbag slung over one shoulder and a massive takeaway coffee in the other hand. Behind her, Rav gave a forced smile and avoided Hudson's eye contact.

Hudson got up and crossed straight to Rav. He shoved the pile of mail at him. "There's more for your security experts to go through. I don't suppose you have any update on yesterday's love letters?"

Rav glanced to Andie for support, before saying, "These things take time." He glanced at the stack. "There's more than ever."

"No shit. And they're just as twisted." He took a deep breath. Flying off the handle was not going to get him anywhere. "Tell your team to look into a guy called Robbie Wiseman."

"Robbie Wiseman, yes. Okay. Who is he?"

"He's sent me stuff similar to this in the past. Most of it was on social media and emails, but there were a handful of letters too. He was obsessed with that same movie. Claimed he wanted to re-enact my death scene with me."

"For real?" Andie said, ditching the bag and joining them. "Where is he now?"

"I've no idea. I did a play in the UK a few years ago and he used to troll me a lot. He'd follow me round the country, get front row seats wherever he could. He'd shout crude remarks during the performance and one night he even followed me to where I was staying."

Rav's eyes widened. "Could he do the same here?"

"We need to check who has bought tickets and see if his name shows up," Andie said.

"I doubt he'll be stupid enough to book in his own name," Hudson said. "We got a stalking order last time. He wasn't allowed anywhere near me, or any of the venues where the show was playing. But I don't know if that will still be in place. It might only have been for the length of that particular play. I never heard from him again afterward."

"If we can prove he sent these" — Rav waved the pile of letters — "we can get something similar."

"It's a start," Hudson said with a sigh.

"You should have mentioned this sooner. We could have done something about it by now." Andie pushed her glasses onto the top of her head.

Hudson remained cool. "Says the woman who hid the fact I'd been receiving this shit for a whole week."

"Yes, yes. Well, we all know now. We can get something done about it. We don't want some nutcase fan of yours turning up on press night and ruining everything."

"Your compassion is overwhelming," he deadpanned.

Andie gave a sarcastic smile and headed back to her handbag.

"That's not everything," Hudson raised his voice. "There's something else you neglected to mention. Like letting reporters sit in on the rehearsals."

She shrugged. "I didn't think it was important. I've been assured we won't even know he's here."

"Don't you thinking having a stranger in the room is going to throw us off our game when we're only beginning to make advances?"

"Why would it? It's one man from the local newspaper, not a fly-on-the-wall documentary crew."

No doubt you'll be keeping that for the London run, if it ever happens. "We don't need it."

"That's where you're wrong," Rav interjected. "We need all the good press we can get. It's not enough to pay for publicity anymore. We need word of mouth. This guy is the first step. He might just be local, but he's good. Respected. If we're going to take this play to the West End, then this Blyham production needs to be a sell-out. Every night — full houses for the entire run. Luke Kamal is an integral part of making that happen."

Hudson sighed. He knew what Rav was saying made sense, but it still rankled. "Couldn't you bring him in for the last few days, or for previews? Why does it have to be now, when the play is in such a raw state?"

"Because that's the angle. He's not just writing a first night review, he's going to cover all aspects. There might even be a book in it if the transfer looks likely," Rav said. "You won't even know he's here."

Little chance of that. Luke's smouldering good looks would be a distraction, anyway, never mind the reason he was here.

Hudson realised there was little to gain by arguing with the producer and the director. Their minds would not be changed, and his energy would be better focused elsewhere. He'd hoped to be in a better mindset ahead of today's run-through, but he'd been wound up about the press sitting in on the rehearsal, and he was not as well prepared as he should be. He took his script and his coffee into the far corner of the room and read through the opening pages. Luckily the dialogue was already fixed in his mind—it was a case now of working out how he wanted to play it.

Luke arrived early, before any of the other performers. Hudson looked up carefully from his script, merely observing, not yet ready to engage. He was too far away to make out what was being said between him and Rav and Andie. Any hopes that they might have sent him away were dismissed when Luke took off his jacket and hung it over the back of a chair.

Shit. He's staying then.

Luke wore jeans and a dark shirt which skimmed the striking contours of his torso. For a reporter, he was clearly very active to have a body as perfect as that. He moved well too, opening a battered leather satchel to take out a laptop, a notebook and pens. Then he glanced across the room and caught Hudson looking straight at him.

Hudson returned his attention to the pages in front of him but found it impossible to concentrate. The words became an indecipherable blur. He realised too late that Luke was walking straight towards him.

"Hi," he said. "I feel like I owe you an apology for last night."

That deep, sexy voice had an unnerving power behind it. Hudson found himself responding. He put down the script. "You weren't to know," he said at last, keeping his own tone firm. He wasn't ready to back down on this matter. From his experience, journalists were not to be trusted. Just because this one came in an attractive package, it didn't make him any better than the rest. "But all the same, I can't pretend to be happy that you're here."

Way to go. Make him hate you from the start so he'll do a real hatchet piece on you in print.

"I'm very excited about this play. About you being in it. I want to assure you that I have nothing but huge respect for everyone involved."

The face, the eyes, the voice, it was almost enough to make Hudson melt. He couldn't resist sneaking a look at his crotch and spotting the noticeable bulge inside his jeans. In an instant, he imagined what it would be like, dropping to his knees and pressing his face against that bulge. Feeling it harden and grow. The dampness that would form in Luke's underwear. *Damn. Why does he have to be a fucking reporter?* Especially when he was so hot.

"I've been burned by your type before," he said, getting his mind out of Luke's crotch, forcing himself to focus on his face.

A smile flickered across his mouth. "My type?"

"You know what I mean. Don't tell me you haven't screwed someone over in print because your story was more sensational that the truth.

He shook his head. "I'm interested in art and theatre, not celebrity gossip. I hope I can convince you of that in the coming days."

Don't crack. "We'll see. If you can stay out of the way, that's good enough for me."

The rest of the team started to arrive, and Luke went over to introduce himself. Hudson wanted to believe he was genuine, mainly because he was so gorgeous, but he'd been badly burned by the press in the past. He wasn't about to lower his guard for a hot piece of ass.

No matter how badly he'd like to get into that ass.

Chapter Four

"He Used to Be a Real Hottie"

Later that night, Hudson found himself outside The Viaduct, the sex bar close to his apartment building, wondering whether to go in. Working with Luke close by all day had got him into a state of sexual frustration, the likes of which he hadn't known in a long time. He had caught Luke glancing in his direction more than once throughout the day, and hadn't been imagining it—he recognised mutual attraction when it stared him in the face. But it was out of the question. Mixing business with pleasure was a disastrous idea, even more so when it involved a dalliance with the enemy.

He knew he was being uncharitable to think of Luke as the bad guy, but if that's what it took to maintain a distance and put a damper on the juvenile lust he felt for him, then that's the way it would stay.

Despite that, he was horny.

Would the answer to his problem lie inside The Viaduct?

Since getting back to the apartment a little after seven, he'd been pacing the floor in a state of frustration. He'd gone for a quick meal after work with Julian at the restaurant within the Concert Hall but had come home alone, unable to get the image of Luke Kamal out of his mind. In the shower, he'd stroked his dick and teased his asshole as he imagined what Luke would look like naked. He'd squirmed in frustration against his slippery fingers, needing to come but unable to finish. In the end he'd turned the dial to cold to dampen his horniness.

After a shower, he'd gone online to see what The Viaduct was really about. It seemed to be a club, set over several floors within the caverns of the ancient railway bridge that ran behind the apartment. It sounded like a fun idea. They hosted various themed nights across the month and tonight's premise was masquerade. Customers were expected to strip fully naked except for a mask over their faces. Masks were available at the door for those who didn't own one of their own.

It sounded a little crazy, but it could be fun. Hot, maybe. Even better, no one would know who he was. *Leading man visits local gay sex dungeon* was not the kind of headline Rav would appreciate for the play. But with a mask covering his face, he could do as he pleased.

Having made up his mind, he'd pulled on jeans and T-shirt and headed out into the balmy summer night.

Only, standing outside The Viaduct, Hudson got cold feet.

Sex clubs had never been his scene. He'd visited a couple when he was younger and had found it a surreal experience. He'd spent more time watching what was going on than participating, usually going after the men who weren't interested in him, while avoiding attention from the ones who were.

As he studied the poster beside the door, a couple of men approached and gave him a thorough looking over before going inside. They were around his age, with well-built, hyper-masculine bodies, but they were kind of intense—scary even—rather than sexy. He wondered if they were all like that inside.

Maybe a drink first, to bolster his courage.

Most of the bars in the area were LGBTQ+ establishments. He'd done some research into the scene and had visited a couple of them last weekend. They'd been packed and he'd only stayed for one drink, feeling out of it on his own. There was a pub not far from The Viaduct that seemed more like a regular place. Hudson headed there first.

Damn Luke Kamal. How could one man have got him so worked up in such a short time?

Hudson heard music playing from outside The New Inn. It was typical upbeat gay bar stuff, and he went in. He was surprised at how busy it was for a Tuesday night, though the patrons were predominantly much younger than he was. Students, he figured.

He ordered a vodka with ice and found a place to stand against the far wall. It seemed like a nice enough bar. The Blue Pearl down by the river was more his kind of place, but he hadn't come out tonight to listen to great music. He was looking for dick.

Unfortunately, none of the men here were to his taste. They hung around in groups, few of them smiling or even talking, fixated on the screens in their hands. There were a handful of more lively men through the open archway, in the other room, but even if Hudson had been their own age, they would not have attracted him. They were too young, too into their phones. *Too unlike Luke.*

Would anyone satisfy him tonight apart from the hot reporter? It seemed unlikely. What a strange situation to find himself in — lusting after the enemy. *Is Luke really the enemy?* Yes. *No.* Hudson no longer knew what to think. All that was certain was how much he wanted to kiss that mouth and ravish that superb body.

"Hi," a man said. Hudson had been so lost in his thoughts, he hadn't seen him approach.

He was a little more mature than the bulk of the people here. Early thirties, maybe? Fair hair, good build. Not too bad overall.

"Hi," Hudson replied.

The man grinned and stepped nearer, a little too close for Hudson's liking, considering they had just met. Some personal space would be appreciated. The man looked him up and down. "Do I know you? You seem familiar. Very."

"I just have one of those faces," Hudson said, slipping into his best English accent. It sounded quite posh, as the Blyham dialect was still beyond him, but his natural American accent would have given too much away. "This is my first time in here. I'm new to Blyham."

There was a flicker of confusion before the man continued. "You do stand out among all these kids." He laughed, gesturing to the crowd behind them. "I wouldn't be in here myself tonight, but I have to work weekends. If I don't come out on my days off, I don't get the fucking chance. What's your name, by the way?"

"Luke," came out of his mouth before he could stop it.

The man looked unconvinced. "Gaz," he said.

It struck Hudson as being equally fake, but what the hell. They weren't looking to make a lasting connection.

Gaz's chest strained against his T-shirt, revealing erect nipples. He was much broader than Luke, thickset all over. Hudson wondered why he was even comparing them. Luke wasn't here. Gaz was.

"I'm probably going to head to The Viaduct next." Gaz's eyes linked with Hudson's as he spoke, making the intention of the words very clear. "You been?"

He shook his head. "Any good?"

"Some nights yes, some nights no. Though if you were there, it would be a lot more fucking hopeful than usual." Gaz gave the bulge in the front of his jeans an enthusiastic grope, delineating the outline of what was inside — concealed but still proudly on display.

Hudson couldn't decide how he felt about Gaz. He wasn't unattractive, far from it, but he was more than a little needy. Hudson wasn't sure how far he wanted to go with this, if he wanted to go anywhere at all. Gaz's biggest problem at this moment was that he wasn't Luke.

Fuck. Have I really got such a hard-on for him?

Gaz's eyes narrowed. "I know where I think I've seen you before. You look like that actor. You know, the one who's going to be doing that play here. Some guys from work have got tickets to see it. He used to be a real hottie."

"Thank you." Hudson laughed.

"You know the American. Oh, what's his name? Matt…Bomer, no, that's not the one. You don't look much like him." He snapped his fingers. "Hudson Rhodes." Then he leaned in even closer. "Actually, you look a *lot* like him. Older, but you could pass for brothers. I used to really fucking fancy him when I was young, you know."

Any spark of interest Hudson might have had in Gaz was rapidly going out.

Undeterred, Gaz carried on. "Have you seen that horror film he was in? The one where he gets chased around in his underpants by the killer?"

Hudson took a strong drink. "I don't watch horror films."

"This is a good one. If only for that scene. There's a bit where his pants get caught and he flashes his arse." Gaz cupped his hands in the air to demonstrate grabbing a feel. "You only see it quickly, but I used to pause the DVD at that exact moment just to get a good look." He pulled out his phone. "I bet I can find it online. I'll show you."

If Hudson had had a hard-on, that was the exact moment he'd have gone soft.

The sexual tension that had built up across the day finally dissipated. He checked his watch. It was almost eleven. If he got out of here soon, he could be in bed by twelve and get a decent night's sleep ahead of tomorrow's day in the studio. He threw back his drink.

"Gaz, it's been really nice to meet, but I'm done in. I'm going to head off now. You have a good night."

Gaz didn't look up from his eager scrolling. "Just a minute. I've almost found it. The film is *Red Hills Massacre*. Wait until you see how hot this guy was."

"Have fun at The Viaduct," Hudson called as he walked away. He couldn't get out of there fast enough.

Chapter Five

A Truce

The next morning, Hudson was in a much better frame of mind. After his failed attempt to explore the gay scene of Blyham for a one-night stand, he'd gone straight back to his apartment.

In bed, he'd spent some time searching through the archives of *The Blyham Chronicle* to see the kind of articles Luke Kamal had written. What Rav had told him about Luke appeared to check out. His reviews of local theatre shows and art exhibitions were intelligent and well-informed. From what he could see, the *Chronicle* was one of the few newspapers outside of London that ran a comprehensive weekly art supplement, and Luke was given plenty of space to embrace his interests and passions.

Hudson had widened his search to look over Luke's social media and was pleased to find it equally professional, with no questionable behaviour or political rantings. He discovered that Luke had also written a non-fiction book about the history of Blyham's Empire Theatre, where *Darkest Blue* would soon be opening. The last thing he did before falling asleep was to order a copy of the book.

When Luke arrived at the rehearsal studio, Hudson decided it was time for them to start again.

"Hi," he greeted him. "Got a minute?"

Luke's dark eyes narrowed warily before he smiled. Even though it was forced, the smile sent a pure rush all through Hudson. "Of course."

"Well, there's no easy way to say this, so I'll just come out with it. I've been behaving like a complete asshole these last few days and I'm sorry. It's not your fault. It's mine. I've had…issues with certain journalists in the past which have tainted my opinion. I shouldn't have assumed you'd be the same."

The smile took on a warmer aspect. "I'm sorry you've had to go through that, but I can assure you I'm not a gossip journalist. I don't look for dirt. Never have, never will."

"I realise that now." Then he admitted, "I've done some homework on you. And it all seems to check out."

Luke laughed openly. "I'm glad to hear it. I meant everything I said yesterday. It's an honour for me to have such privileged access to this production and I want nothing but the best for this play and the theatre. This is a big deal for me."

They were among the first to arrive that morning. Manuella and Steve Dillard, who played the other male lead, were also late, but even Julian had yet to make an appearance. Andie and Rav had their heads together with a set designer.

"Do you feel like getting a proper coffee before we start?" Hudson suggested.

"Absolutely."

There was a large coffee shop in the foyer of the Concert Hall. Hudson breathed in the gorgeous scent of Luke's cologne as they walked down to the front. Now that he had given himself permission to like Luke, he was suddenly all in.

Luke was a good few inches taller than him. Hudson kept stealing glances as they progressed. His profile was just as strong as his front view, the chin, the nose, the thick dark hair. All very masculine. Very handsome.

"I see you wrote a book about the theatre we're moving into."

Luke gave him a side glance. He was smiling. "You really have done your research."

"I'm sure you have, too," he replied with good nature.

"Guilty. But not just on you. I've done a deep dive into all aspects of the show, cast and creatives."

"Will all of that go into your articles?"

"Oh God, no. It's just how my brain works." He tapped his forehead. "I need to get it all locked in up here before I can make progress. I'm sure you're the same when you play a character. I can't get started until I know it all inside out."

When they arrived at the coffee shop, the sun reflected off the still waters of the river. It was almost a mirror for the change in Hudson's mood, and how much his attitude had altered since yesterday. They placed their orders and waited at the end of the counter for them to be fixed.

Luke wore dark trousers and a white open-necked shirt. The colour contrasted perfectly with his light brown skin tone. With the top two buttons undone, Hudson stole a peek at the hair on his impressive chest.

He imagined following the trail of hair lower, seeing where it would lead.

"How are you finding our city?" Luke asked.

"I haven't had a lot of free time to explore it yet. But I like what I've seen so far."

"You've come at the best time, in summer. The winters are cold and bleak, but thankfully we have plenty to keep us busy. For a small city, there's a lot to do."

"Have you lived here for long?"

His brow furrowed in thought. "Just over eight years. I grew up not far from here in Newcastle, and went to uni in Nottingham. I got my first job in Manchester, then moved to a newspaper in Leeds, before finally making it to Blyham. When I was young, I found it quite dull compared to those bigger cities, but I love it now. Wouldn't want to live anywhere else."

Hudson dragged his gaze away from Luke to look out of the window. "I can see why."

"If you'd like a guide to show you around…"

Now their eyes were locked on each other again. Hudson was certain he was not misreading the signals. There was something between them. "I'd like that," he said. "A lot."

"How about we start on familiar ground? There's a great duo performing at The Blue Pearl tonight. I'm planning to check them out, if you'd like to join me? They play kind of electropop, if you're into that kind of thing. I saw them earlier in the year and they were brilliant."

His accent was so cute. Hudson adored the way he said brilliant, his voice rising on the second half of the word. "I'd love to. How about we go early and get a bite to eat first?"

"Even better."

Hudson had loose plans to go out with Julian at the end of the day, but doubted his co-star would object, given how close he seemed to be getting to leading lady Manuella.

The drinks arrived. Hudson waited while Luke emptied a sachet of brown sugar into his takeaway cup and gave it a good stir. He had strong hands with long fingers. His forearms and the backs of his hands were coated in fine black hairs.

Once again, Hudson found himself fantasising about the rest of Luke's body. *I bet he's got a really pretty, hairy ass.*

If the budding chemistry between them continued to develop, maybe he would find out. There was no hurry. Hudson knew better than to rush it. After all, he'd only called a truce with Luke about twenty minutes ago.

The good-natured chat continued on the walk back up to the rehearsal room. Luke asked gentle questions about Hudson's feelings for the play so far and what had drawn him to the character.

"If I'm honest, I just love working on stage these days. Far more than all those low-budget movies I get offered. The week before last, I flew to Romania to shoot for three days on a movie that most likely won't ever get released, at least not widely. It might get dumped on a streaming service someday. The seven weeks I've committed to *Darkest Blue* are so much more satisfying than that."

"Surely it's going to be a lot longer than seven weeks. If the play goes to London, it could be a good six months or more."

"If it happens. I don't take anything for granted. Right now, I've got a guaranteed contract for the Blyham run. Nothing more certain than that."

"I think it will do well," Luke said. "The script is incredible. The cast is perfect, and the tickets are already selling well."

"None of that counts for anything without great word of mouth. If the public don't love the show, we'll be going nowhere."

When they arrived back upstairs, Manuella and Steve had at last turned up, though the beautiful Spanish actress was engrossed in her phone. Steve Dillard was showing off to the production assistants.

Hudson had yet to make up his mind about his young co-star. Steve had dark, sexy good looks, but he was also ambitious and very vain. He'd had a breakthrough role the year before in a Netflix drama show and seemed to think he was real hot shit because of it. He'd already been brutal in his opinion that he didn't think he should have a less prominent position on the *Darkest Blue* poster to an "American has-been".

He was an immature asshole. Hudson didn't think he should hold that against him, though. He'd been the same after his first taste of success, too.

"Time for me to become invisible," Luke said. "Catch you later."

He gave Hudson a light pat on the shoulder. That mere touch sent a thrill right through his body, which ended in a tingling sensation in his nuts. *God damn.* That was electric.

Luke retreated to a chair against the far wall from where he would observe. If he thought he was going to go unnoticed, he was very wrong. Hudson couldn't take his eyes off him.

Snap out of it. He had to get his shit together. Put the play first. For the next six or seven hours, that's the only thing that should matter. He could pick things up with this major hottie when they had dinner together later.

Hudson went over to the group of actors. He could see straight away that they were still short. Julian was missing. It was unlike him to be late.

"Has anyone heard from Julian today?" he asked.

"I've tried calling," Manuella said, looking up from her phone screen. "No reply."

Hudson checked his own phone to see if there were any messages. Nothing.

"He could be just stuck on transport," Andie said, glancing at her watch. "Though he should have set off in good time. A ten o'clock call is hardly the crack of dawn."

"That can't be it. He walks in every day. He's staying just five minutes away."

Andie sucked her teeth before summoning a production assistant. The young girl, Ruth, seemed terrified of her. "Go round to his place and knock his lazy arse out of bed. You'll find the address in the database." She turned her attention back to the cast. "No point in waiting. He doesn't appear until twenty-five minutes in. Let's go with a run-through of Act One, from the top."

Apart from Steve fluffing several of his lines and Manuella freezing at one point, the rehearsal went well. Ruth had not returned with Julian by the time his character made his entrance, so Andie stepped in to read his dialogue. They made it all the way to the end of the act without stopping.

"Pretty good," Andie declared when they were done. "Not great, but better than decent." She called a ten-minute break before they would start work on Act Two.

Ruth returned during the break, without Julian. She spoke meekly to Andie, whose face darkened in fury.

"What's up?" Hudson asked.

"I can't find him," Ruth said, shrinking under Andie's glare. "There was no answer at the door."

"Couldn't reception put a call through?" Andie asked.

"He's in an Airbnb," Hudson said. "There isn't a reception." This was totally out of character for the seasoned actor. They had only known each other a short time, but Julian came across as a total professional, and his lengthy list of credits spoke for themselves. "I think we should start checking local hospitals. And someone needs to reach the Airbnb owners and get in there to make sure he's okay."

"He's probably shacked up with some slapper and sleeping off a hangover," Steve said with a dirty chuckle.

Hudson shot him a look. *Little prick.* "No fucking way. He's not like that and you know it. Something must be wrong for him to go AWOL."

Reluctantly, Andie set Ruth to work trying to contact someone with a key to Julian's apartment and calling the local hospitals to check admissions. "If he turns up hungover, he can forget all about playing your understudy," Andie snapped at Hudson. "He'll have his bit part and nothing more."

Her lack of compassion was a total pisser, but Hudson was in no mood for an argument with her. He was more concerned about his friend.

Hudson checked his own phone again and, finding no texts from Julian, called his number. There was still no answer. He left a voice mail letting him know he was concerned and to get in touch immediately. Hudson already had an uneasy feeling. He'd always had a good sense of when something was off, and Julian's absence triggered that familiar sensation.

He glanced towards Luke, who raised a reassuring smile. He seemed intent to sit the moment out. Whatever was happening was between the cast and had nothing to do with his article. Hudson was grateful that he didn't try to interfere for a piece of juicy gossip.

Andie insisted that everyone get back to work on the beginning of Act Two. "We don't have the luxury of time. Let's get this nailed down."

They had been at it for less than five minutes when Hudson became aware of a commotion at the back of the room. Two uniformed police officers had appeared and were talking to Rav. Andie tried to keep the read-through going but lost the will of the cast. Hudson's insides were already turning in knots. He shot her a stern look before abandoning the read-through and heading straight towards Rav and the cops.

"What's going on?" he asked. A small part of him clung to the prospect that Julian had got shitfaced last night and was currently sleeping it off in a police cell. It was a slim hope, and it evaporated in an instant when he saw the look on Rav's face.

"It's Julian," the producer faltered. "They...they found a body in a back alley this morning and think it might be him. They think Julian is dead."

Chapter Six

Julian

At first there was silence, followed by gasps of shock all around the room. Murmuring and questions then statements of disbelief. Hudson dropped onto the nearest chair, gripping the armrests for additional support. It took a full minute for what Rav had said to sink in.

"He was found dead in a back alley," he said numbly, staring between the producer and the two police officers. "*Found dead*? Do you mean he was killed? Murdered?"

"All lines of enquiry are open at the moment," one of the cops, a young blond guy with a receding hairline, said.

"If he was found in an alley, then it's unlikely he dropped down dead of natural causes," Hudson said.

"We need to speak to everyone here," the second officer said. "CID will be along soon, but we need to get started with your initial statements."

"We're in the middle of rehearsals." Andie had the good grace to look appalled at her own words as soon as they were out of her mouth. "Sorry. Of course. Yes."

A long, low moaning sound started behind him, quickly turning into a heartfelt wail. It was Manuella. She sat with her hands raised beside her head, her mouth wide as her anguish poured out. Andie and a couple of the team rushed to her, but she seemed utterly inconsolable. Tears ran down her face and dripped off her chin. Hudson hadn't realised how close she'd got to Julian. Maybe things had been more serious between them than Julian had let on.

Steven held his phone in a two-handed grip and tapped at the screen with both thumbs.

Rav stood open-mouthed, gawping at the police officers without a sound coming out. Hudson realised he would have to take charge.

"Has anyone told his family yet?" he asked.

"We were hoping you could provide us with their contact information," the blond cop said.

"Absolutely." He gestured for Ruth. "You know how to get into the personal files on Andie's laptop. Pull up Julian's details right away."

She nodded, seemingly grateful to have something to do.

"Who knew Mr King the best?" the second cop asked.

"I did, I guess. And Manuella."

The leading lady was in no condition to give a statement at that moment, so while one cop found out what they needed to know from Ruth, he sat down with the blond officer, PC Jenkinson. Hudson told him everything he knew about Julian.

"We only met a couple of weeks ago, but we hit it off straight away. He's also understudying my part, so we've been helping each other with the lines. *Fuck*." It hit him in that moment that Julian was dead, and he wouldn't do any of that again. No opening night celebrations. No anxious wait for the first reviews. For Julian, there was nothing. "Are you *sure* it's him? Could there be a mistake?"

"How likely is it he wouldn't show up for work?"

"Not at all."

"There you go then. We haven't made a positive ID yet, but we're ninety-nine per cent certain. When did you see him last?"

"Last night, when we finished here. We often go for food afterward. It was nothing special. Just a quick bite at the restaurant downstairs. We left before seven."

"Did he know anyone else in the city? Someone he could have met with?"

"He had a bit of a thing going with Manuella. They sometimes saw each other on an evening, but I can't say about last night. He didn't mention it."

"Did he ever talk about anyone else? Besides those connected with the play?"

Hudson shrugged. "He never mentioned meeting anyone, so I doubt it. I think the whole cast and creative team are from out of town. None of us are local to the city."

"Did he ever mention having trouble with anyone? Any issues he was worried about?"

"Julian? Absolutely not. He's one of the nicest guys I've ever worked with. I don't think you'll find a single person here with a bad word to say about him."

He wondered if he should mention his own hate mail, then decided against it. It was his problem and had nothing to do with Julian. Besides, none of it was particularly threatening. It was just creepy shit from some anonymous rando. They were rarely the kind of person to put themselves in the way of any kind of confrontation.

"You can't seriously think it was someone in this room. Can you tell me anything about what happened?" Hudson asked. "Was it a mugging, mistaken identity? Wrong place, wrong time?"

"I'm not at liberty to say at the moment, sir. But as soon as my CID colleagues arrive, I'm sure they'll have further information for you."

They did not have to wait for the investigation team to arrive to find out more. Luke was already one step ahead. When the police moved on to interview other members of the cast, Luke approached Hudson, Rav and Andie. He had his phone in his hand.

"It's not my department, but I have friends at the paper who are already on the case. Nothing official yet, but they've managed to talk to people who were on the scene first. A delivery driver found a body in an alley on the other side of the river around six a.m."

"Shit," Hudson said.

"The guy got a mighty fright. From what I hear, it was no accident. The body was in quite a state when he was discovered."

"What does that mean?" Andie asked.

Luke lowered his voice further. "They're saying there were stab wounds. The body was badly mutilated and there was blood all over the alley."

Hudson's head was light again. This sounded more like something from one of his shitty old horror films than reality.

"And it's definitely Julian?" he asked.

"I've no idea," Luke said. He pointed at the two police officers. "But the fact they're here must mean they think so."

"I don't get it," Rav said. "Who would want to attack Julian? And so brutally."

Luke grimaced. "It's clear none of you are too familiar with Blyham. This hasn't been the safest city to live in for some time. Wandering around after dark is not recommended, especially to someone on their own."

"So, what are you saying?" Hudson asked. "Could it be a street robbery gone wrong?"

Luke spread his hands and shrugged. "I couldn't hazard a guess right now. If you do a search of the crime rate here for the last two years, you'll see exactly what I mean. Blyham might be a small city, but it's got problems as severe as any capital."

* * * *

The police didn't want anyone to leave until the CID officers had interviewed them. Manuella was now hysterical, being comforted by several of the team. At a loss for anything else to do, Hudson and Luke returned to the coffee shop. He'd told Andie to call them if the cops arrived before they got back. Luke kept checking the messages on his phone, but he had nothing new to report.

They sat together at a table towards the rear. The last thing Hudson wanted now was to get recognised and have to answer questions.

"How long do you think it will be before the press realise who has been killed and turn up here?"

"I haven't mentioned it to anyone at the paper," Luke said defensively, "if that's what you're getting at."

"I'm not," Hudson said wearily. He couldn't blame Luke for being wary after the way he'd behaved. "I just...need to prepare myself for the worst."

Luke put his elbows on the table and leant forward a little. He pursed his lips before speaking. "Why do you have so much hate for the media?"

"I thought you said you'd done a lot of research. You don't have to Google me for long to understand why."

"Is it because of when you came out? I wasn't following at the time, but it seemed to get a lot of attention, especially in the States."

"I didn't come out. I was outed. Thrown to the wolves, in fact, to save someone else's career."

"I'm sorry. I can't believe that still goes on."

Hudson shrugged. "It's a while ago. A different era. I don't want to talk about it now. Can we change the subject?"

Luke nodded. His dark brown eyes were deep and warm. The more Hudson looked at him, the more incredibly attractive he became. Those eyes, the fine, straight nose, that wide mouth.

"Does Julian have any family?" Luke asked.

"He's single right now, apart from whatever was blossoming between him and Manuella. I don't know if he's been married before or whether there are any kids. He was in his mid-thirties, so if there are kids, they'll be pretty young. He told me his parents have a family-run restaurant. Whenever the acting work ran dry, he would help out there."

Luke sighed. "They'll be receiving the knock at the door that no one ever wants to receive."

Hudson picked up his phone and pulled up Julian's credits. There was a vast gallery of images, going way back to his youth theatre days. He hadn't changed all that much over the years, except to get more distinguished and handsome. "He's done a lot of great things. Drama, musicals, comedy. His TV credits are pretty incredible."

"Yeah," Luke agreed. "He's appeared in at least one episode of just about every major British TV show there is. Often just a scene or two, but he always made a huge impression. I've never understood why he wasn't a bigger star. I saw him in a production down in London a year or so ago. He was magnetic on stage. I was surprised when I saw he had such a small role in *Darkest Blue.*"

"Very few actors get to choose the roles they play. Most of the time we just take what we can get. Julian doesn't appear to have any big ego…" Hudson corrected himself. "Didn't. *Fuck.* I can't believe this." He wrung his hands. "I keep expecting to wake up."

"I'm sorry. I can see you'd become good friends."

"What was that you were saying earlier? About the crime rate in Blyham."

"It's off the fucking chart," Luke said. "I can't believe none of you guys knew. These last few years have been appalling. When I first moved here, things were pretty good. There would occasionally be trouble on a weekend when you'd get large groups of out-of-town people coming in to party. Blyham has always had a reputation as a party hotspot. But it quickly got worse. Antisocial behaviour increased, and then hate crime rocketed. Racism, homophobia, transphobia. Things have been very dicey around the gay village area for a couple of years. There's not a single weekend when at least one person doesn't get queer-bashed."

Hudson stared at him in disbelief. "You're shitting me. I'm renting an apartment right in the middle of the area and I haven't seen anything."

"Have you been going out late on Fridays and Saturdays?"

"No, I've barely been out at all."

"Then you've managed to escape it. I would suggest you look up the Blyham Strangler when you have a chance, though it might not be the best idea if you want to sleep well. I'm pleased to say he's now in prison where he belongs. But there's lots of other dangerous people still around. The violence didn't stop after he was put away."

"Surely that's not what happened to Julian. He's white, straight. He doesn't tick any of the boxes for the kind of hate crimes you're talking about."

Luke took a mouthful of coffee and put the cup down thoughtfully. "No, but he dresses well, speaks with quite a posh accent. For Blyham, anyway. He'd stand out for being different, and sometimes that's all it takes."

Ruth appeared over Luke's shoulder, scanning the room. She appeared more stressed than he'd ever seen her. Hudson raised his hand and waved at her.

"Hey, looking for us?"

She rushed over, relief written all over her face. "Yes, Hudson. Andie sent me to find you." She glanced around, checking who was in earshot then lowered her voice. "The CID team have arrived. They want to speak to you."

"Give me five minutes to finish my coffee and use the bathroom and I'll be right there."

She smiled nervously and hurried away.

"CID are here," Luke said. "I guess that confirms it. They must have ID'd Julian."

As his stomach churned, Hudson pushed his half-finished drink away, no longer interested.

"What about you?" he asked. "You told me you've been here eight years. If Blyham is so bad, why do you stay around?"

Luke smiled softly. "Despite everything, I still love the place. I love my job, the theatre, the culture. I'm not going to be driven away by a bunch of arseholes so unhappy in their own lives they need to make life a misery for everyone else."

"You live here in the city?"

He laughed. "Fuck no. I don't love it that much. I have a house along the coast. It's only a twenty-minute drive in good traffic, but it's far enough away to feel like another place entirely."

"That sounds cool." Hudson stuffed his phone in his pocket and made a move to get up. He paused. "Do you still feel like getting a drink tonight? I totally understand if you don't, but after this, I really don't fancy a night on my own in that apartment. I'd appreciate some company."

Luke's smile brightened the grim mood. "I'd love to. To be honest, I was hoping you'd say that. I don't fancy spending an evening on my own either."

"I take it that means you're single?"

"Well, obviously. I wouldn't be going on a date with a hot leading man otherwise."

Now Hudson smiled. He could feel the heat rising over his face, colouring his cheeks. "It's a date?"

Luke raised an eyebrow. "If it's not, I'll be more than a little disappointed. But given everything that's going on, let's keep it low-key."

"Low-key suits me."

He gave Luke a gentle pat on the shoulder as he walked away.

He was filled with dread as he went off to speak to the police officers, but at least he had something to look forward to at the end of the day. Then a shard of guilt lanced through him.

Poor Julian wouldn't look forward to anything ever again.

Chapter Seven

An Evening at Home

Hudson turned his face into the full force of the shower faucet and surrendered, allowing the heat and pressure to ease some of the tension that had developed across the day. An hour-long neck and back massage with a sports therapist would be great right now but he had to make do with the water. He rolled his head and shrugged his shoulders, breathing deeply.

What a day.

By the time he'd finally left the rehearsal studios at seven, the stage door had been crowded with reporters and photographers. A riot of opportunistic chaos. Rav had already put out a statement on behalf of the team but that hadn't been enough to placate the demand for news and gossip. Thankfully, Rav had also arranged a car for him, and he'd dived into the back seat and kept his gaze fixed straight ahead as they'd pulled away. Of all the garbled questions he'd heard in the few moments it took to get from the door to the car, not one of them had mentioned Julian.

"Is the production jinxed...? Will the play go ahead...? Are you going back to America...? Do you think you'll be next...?"

Fucking piranhas.

Ordinarily he would never have considered taking a car for a journey that took ten minutes to walk, but as they approached his building and he'd seen another band of reporters waiting, he'd been grateful that Rav had had the foresight to arrange one. The driver got him as close to the door as possible. Hudson had managed to say something about how much Julian had meant to him and how devasted he was for his family before shoving his way inside.

Now, his temporary home was no longer a sanctuary.

Hudson scrubbed his body from top to bottom, paying close attention his cock, balls and ass. He had no real expectation that his evening with Luke would amount to anything more than company, but it would boost his confidence to know he was squeaky clean anyway.

As he stepped out of the shower, he heard the doorbell.

He checked the time. *Shit.*

He grabbed a towel, wrapped it around his waist and hurried out of the bathroom.

Luke's eyes widened in surprise when he opened the door.

"Am I early?"

"No. Sorry. It's me. I think I've just spent a full twenty minutes in the shower. Come in."

He was aware of the attention Luke paid to his body and suddenly felt very self-conscious standing there still wet. His nipples had hardened and stood erect through his chest hair. This was not how he'd intended for the evening to start. He tightened the towel around his waist, suddenly aware of another burgeoning erection.

"How was it downstairs?" he asked as Luke followed him into the room. "Are the reporters still there?"

He couldn't help wondering if Luke was looking at his ass.

"There are five of them still hanging around. They were speaking to someone who might be one of your neighbours."

"Well, I don't really know anyone in the building so there's nothing they can tell them."

"Those guys looked pretty pissed off when I came inside. They must think I have some kind of exclusive." Luke raised a takeaway carrier. "I didn't know what you'd want so I got a selection of Italian food. It can all be reheated whenever you're ready."

"Thanks. Why don't you fix us both a drink and I'll get dressed? There's beer and wine in the fridge over there. Vodka and whisky in the bottom cupboard."

"Oh," Luke said with a cheeky grin. "I'm disappointed. I thought you were dressed for the evening."

Hudson smiled back, a frisson going all through his body and tingling in his cock. "At least let me get dried."

"Ha, yes. It's probably best that you do. What do you want to drink?"

"I'll have a glass of wine. There's chardonnay in the refrigerator door."

Hudson went into the bedroom, still grinning.

When the mass of journalists had descended on the Concert Hall, he'd known there was no chance of them ever going out for a quiet meal as they had planned. When he'd asked Luke to rearrange the date, it was Luke who had suggested picking up some takeaway food and spending the night in.

"I need to head back to the office for a while," he'd said. "I can collect something for dinner once I'm done."

Hudson had been grateful for the offer. He'd go mad if he'd had to spend an evening hiding in here alone.

He pulled the towel from his waist to dry his hair and was surprised to find his dick at full mast. It seemed incredible that he could be turned on after the kind of day he'd been through, but Luke was having that effect on him. The man's charisma and sex appeal were so overwhelming.

He hurriedly towelled off, then put on deodorant and cologne, before deciding what to wear. Luke was still in the clothes he'd been wearing all day. It would look off if Hudson went all out in a fancy outfit. He pulled on a pair of jeans without underwear, stuffing his now semi-hard cock inside, and a white shirt, leaving the top three buttons undone.

He was almost at the door when he paused, glancing back to his bedside table. Impelled by a deep impulse, he hurried back over and unfastened his jeans. In the top drawer was a selection of stainless-steel cock rings of varying weights and thickness, and a bunch of leather straps. He pulled out a strap and looped it under his balls then around his cock, fastening it tight. He immediately got harder. There was no certainty that this evening with Luke would lead anywhere, but the strap gave an instant boost to his confidence. He adored the tightness around his ball sac, how it lifted and pushed his junk forward.

The linen shirt fell loosely over his groin, concealing the enhancement. Luke would only see what Hudson chose to reveal.

Luke was standing by the window when he came out. He looked so handsome in the evening light. There were two glasses of wine on the coffee table.

"Very nice," he said, taking in Hudson's attire. "Though I think I preferred what you had on when I came in."

It had been a long time since Hudson had met a guy who was so confident and self-assured without being a total asshole.

"I'm glad you came," Hudson said, sweeping up a wine glass. All at once he felt self-conscious and off kilter. Yesterday, he'd hated Luke and now here he was in his living room coming on strong.

Luke, seeming to sense his unease, changed the subject. "I hope you don't mind, but I put the food in your oven on low. It will keep warm for a couple of hours without spoiling."

"Thank you. I've barely eaten all day and I'm still not hungry."

"It's understandable." Luke picked up his glass and sipped. "Fancy stepping outside? It's a lovely night still, and I don't think those journos downstairs will see if you stand back from the edge."

Hudson nodded and followed him onto the balcony. There was a small table and two chairs. He took Luke's advice and pulled them closer to the window before sitting down. The sky was streaked with shades of cobalt, magenta and cerulean blue. The temperature was surprisingly balmy. Hudson had spent so much of the day cooped up indoors, he hadn't appreciated it until now.

"This is the first time I've had anyone up since I arrived," he said.

Luke sat beside him. "How are you feeling now? Knackered, I imagine."

"Dazed and confused is more like it."

"How did it go this afternoon?"

"Rav and Andie are still trying to figure it out. My agent is coming up from London in the morning. I've no idea if we'll continue with the play or whether the entire production will be canned. There are no rehearsals tomorrow, I know that much at least."

"I'm not aware of this ever happening before. Actors have died during production periods of other plays and the show has continued, but when it's part of an ongoing murder investigation, well, I could be wrong, but I think it's unprecedented."

Hudson groaned and took another swallow of wine. "Did you hear anything further when you were in your office?"

"Only to confirm what we already knew. Julian was found in an alley along the quayside, not too far from The Blue Pearl, in fact. The roads are still closed off down that way. He appeared to have been stabbed, and multiple witnesses have confirmed there was a lot of blood at the scene." Luke exhaled. "While I was in the office, I wrote up a tribute article and retrospective on his career. It should be live on the website already and will go out in the print edition tomorrow. I think people will be genuinely surprised when they learn just how many things he'd been in. He's one of those actors who everyone will recognise by his face without necessarily knowing his name."

"They'll know his name for the wrong reasons now. But thank you, for writing what you have."

"How is Manuella?"

"She calmed down enough to give the police a statement. They had a few drinks together last night, and then Julian took her back to her hotel around eleven. I don't think they'd gone any further than a mild flirtation, but the news seems to have hit her hard."

"That should all be covered by the CCTV at her hotel, so it will give the police a starting point for tracing Julian's movements afterwards."

"I hadn't even thought of that." Hudson had finished his glass. He got up. "Might as well bring the whole damn bottle out. That first drink didn't touch the sides."

Luke was leaning over the balcony, looking out when Hudson returned. *Man, that ass is so fine. Just like the rest of him.*

"I think they've finally got the message down there," Luke said. "I can't see anyone at the main entrance now. Maybe one of your neighbours had enough and has moved them on."

Hudson sat and refreshed their glasses. "I don't know why they were even there. We made it clear this afternoon that we wouldn't be making any further statements until tomorrow."

Luke turned to face him, leaning against the balcony rail. Hudson's eyes roamed all over his body before he forced his attention back to Luke's face. He had to get a grip. His behaviour was so inappropriate.

"I didn't recognise any of the reporters when I came in," Luke said. "They must be from the nationals. They're not local guys. This is a big story."

Hudson grimaced.

"I'd love to know what happened to make you so anti-press," Luke said. "But tonight is not the time for you to share it. Right?"

Any other reporter and Hudson would have guessed he was fishing for a lead, but for better or worse, he was already starting to trust Luke. He didn't think that's what was happening here, but even still. "No. I'll tell you about it some time, but not tonight."

Luke held his gaze. "Okay."

"Can we change the subject for a while? My brain feels like it will implode if I talk about this much more."

"Sure thing." Luke jerked his head backwards. "I didn't realise at first, but you're right above The Viaduct here. I don't suppose you even know what that place is yet." He gently bit his top lip.

"I haven't had time to explore the nightlife but I'm not blind," Hudson said. "I've seen the lines to get into that place." His cock was swelling again. He carefully crossed his legs. "Are you familiar with it?"

"I've been a few times. I know a lot of guys who turn their noses up at places like that, but I don't have a problem. After a messy divorce, I found having sex with strangers to be far more desirable than going on dates when I had no interest in another relationship just yet."

"What's it like? The Viaduct?"

"To tell the truth, I don't have experience of any other sex clubs to compare it with. But it's well run, it's clean. It's safe. After the last few years in Blyham, it's a damn sight safer than taking a guy home or hooking up with someone on an app. There's security staff. Other people. A community."

Luke sat beside him again. His long legs were stretched in front of him, crossed at the ankle. "How was that for a change of subject?" His dark eyes shone with good humour.

Hudson would only have to move his leg an inch or two to the left for them to be touching. He resisted the temptation. Inside his jeans, he was throbbing, his mind full of images and scenes, of meeting Luke in that club and taking him into the shadows. "Tell me about yourself."

Luke grinned at him sideways. "There's not a lot to say. I think you know most of it already."

"Not really. You've only talked about your career. Tell me something about you."

Luke adjusted his seat so they were facing each other. He screwed up his eyes, as though giving it some thought. "All right. I'm thirty-eight. I'm single. My family are originally from Morocco, but they moved to the UK three years before I was born, so this is all I've ever known. I've got an older sister and a younger brother. My dad's a doctor, my mother's an art teacher. Is this the kind of thing you wanted to know?"

"Actually, it is," Hudson said. He'd been pretty close in guessing Luke's age and his sexy regional accent made it clear that he'd grown up in this area of England.

"Okay." He sipped his wine and gazed at the sky before continuing. "Oh, what the hell. You already know I'm divorced. Might as well get that skeleton fully out of the closet. It was a short-lived marriage that proved nothing other than I had lousy taste in men for a while."

"We've all got a past," Hudson said. "And lots of mistakes."

"Hmm, we do. I live alone now. I enjoy it that way. When I'm not working, I like a bit of time by myself to decompress and tune out the noise of life. That's why I prefer living along the coast rather than here in the city. You're never really alone in a place like Blyham. There're always too many people around."

"I get that too," Hudson said. "I spend so much time as part of a big team, I need my own space at the end of the day… Until tonight anyway. I'm grateful you came over. This is one time I didn't want to be alone."

Now Luke's expression was serious. "Me neither. I'm glad you agreed to it. I've been flippant until now but I'm serious. More than anything, I'm glad that you're prepared to trust me." He reached across and took hold of Hudson's hand. The gesture came as a shock, but the touch sent a thrill shooting all the way through his body.

"Thanks," Hudson said. He leaned in closer. Close enough to smell him. To feel the heat of his body.

Then he put a hand on the back of Luke's head and drew their mouths together. When their lips touched and their tongues pressed against each other, all Hudson's concerns shrank away. This man, and what was happening between them, was the only thing that mattered.

Chapter Eight

Getting Physical

Hudson stood and raised the tails of his loose-fitting shirt, revealing the full extent of his arousal beneath. Luke didn't hesitate, cupping his cock and balls through his jeans and murmuring appreciatively.

"We should go inside," Hudson said. "Just in case any of those photographers are still hanging around with a high-powered camera."

Luke got up and kissed him on the mouth again. "Lead the way. I can't wait to find out what you've got on under there."

Luke was behind him, his hands on his waist as they walked back into the apartment.

Once inside, Luke wrapped his arms around him, pressing into his back, demonstrating his own hardness. One hand felt for Hudson's cock, while the other explored his firm abdomen. Hudson groaned. He arched his back and leaned into Luke. Luke's breath was hot on the nape of his neck, then his tongue grazed the skin, sending shivers through his body and causing his skin to ripple with gooseflesh. Hudson pressed his ass against Luke's bulge.

"That's hot," he said.

"You're hot," Luke replied, kissing his neck all the while.

A tiny part of his brain said what they were doing was wrong. His friend had died that day, but Hudson knew from experience that death, especially when it was sudden, caused people to react in strange ways. The hunger for sex could be overwhelming. To laugh at death and recklessly defy it by fucking in its face.

Luke's fingers worked their way down the buttons of his shirt. "I want to see you," he whispered. "I want to see all of you."

Luke eased the shirt from Hudson's shoulders and turned him around.

"You've already seen this," Hudson said with a grin.

"I didn't get the chance to fully appreciate before." Luke's hands slipped upwards from his waist, following the plane of his stomach, exploring his hairy chest. Despite hard work, it was not the body he'd had when he was young, when he'd run around in horror movies in just his underwear, but Hudson knew he was good for his age. He didn't care that there was a softness to his belly now. The regime involved in achieving and maintaining a six-pack had been miserable. As Luke investigated his body with undisguised lust, Hudson felt more desired than he had in a long time.

Luke leant forward and buried his face in Hudson's chest, brushing his lips against the hair. He was taller than Hudson and had to stoop. He gripped Hudson's ass in both hands and lifted him towards him. Hudson slipped his arms over Luke's shoulders, feeling the strong muscles beneath his shirt. Luke's mouth found his left nipple, sucking, squeezing with his teeth until it was hard and stiff, then moving to the right.

"Yes," Hudson gasped. He wondered when the right time would be to tell him that he liked things rough. Maybe not just yet. *Let's see how this goes.*

When Luke had his nipples good and hard, he took a step back. His face was flushed, his lips red and wet. "Now I want to see the rest of you."

Hudson spread his arms, opening his posture to give full access. "I'm all yours."

"I've wanted to hear those words from the moment I saw you."

Luke unfastened Hudson's jeans and shoved them down. They fell around his ankles and Hudson raised one foot at a time to step out of them, standing before Luke in nothing but a leather strap, fastened around his balls.

"Wow," Luke said. "Very nice."

He ran his fingertips across the underside of Hudson's smooth balls, causing his cock to twitch. Veins bulged all along the shaft and the muscles in his abdominals tightened involuntarily. Luke gave his balls a gentle slap, testing him. Hudson grunted and stiffened further when Luke took his balls in a firm grip and squeezed.

"I think I'm getting a feel for what you're into."

"You're doing everything right," Hudson told him.

The fact that he was completely naked while Luke remained clothed only turned him on further. He wondered how wild it would be to explore The Viaduct with Luke. How crazy they could get together.

"Shit," he says. "Just remembered. I don't have any condoms."

Luke tugged his balls downwards, stretching the sack. The ache was incredible.

"I don't have any with me either. Let's not worry about that now. There's plenty of other things we can do this evening. And hopefully we'll get the chance to take things further another time." Luke put his hands on Hudson's shoulders. "Now turn around and let me see the rest of you."

Luke's hands maintained the contact while Hudson followed his instructions.

"Oh, yes. That's a really nice arse."

Luke caressed his shoulders, sliding down the curve of Hudson's spine until he cupped his butt cheeks in both hands. He squeezed and lifted, feeling the weight and firmness of his flesh. Luke pressed his chest against Hudson's back. With his mouth close to his ear, he spread his buttocks apart, and pressed his bulge into the cleft, letting Hudson feel his hardness.

Hudson ground his ass against him.

"Is that what you're into?" Luke asked.

"Mmm," Hudson said. "I'm versatile. I like to fuck every way. It just depends on the vibe of the man I'm with."

Luke's hands were around the front again. One hand squeezing his nuts, the other stroking his shaft. "That makes two of us. I like a guy who doesn't impose any rules."

Luke's fingers were like magic as they glided over him. "Easy," Hudson gasped. "I'm on a hair trigger."

Luke turned him around to face him again.

In the fading light of the room, Luke's eyes were dark, sensual pools. He pushed Hudson backwards until his bare ass pressed against the cool leather of the sofa, then dropped to his knees. The head of Hudson's cock glistened with pre-cum. Luke licked the tip, savouring the taste for a moment before swallowing. Then he took Hudson's cock in his mouth, working fast until the whole of the shaft was rooted in his throat.

"Holy shit!"

Luke deep-throated with ease, taking all of him. Hudson's balls, held forward by the strap, pressed against his chin with each forward thrust. Hudson placed both hands on the edge of the sofa as his thighs trembled with pleasure.

Every sensation was magnified by the leather, tightening his balls and cock, making him infinitely aware of Luke's mouth, tongue and throat. Luke put his hands on Hudson's thighs, widening them, before sliding a finger into the tight crack of his ass. Hudson tilted his hips, making it easier for him. Luke located his hole, stroked the outer rim, moist with sweat, and pressed inside.

"Oh, Christ."

What had already been an incredibly intense experience intensified. Luke pressed into him, while working Hudson's cock with his expert mouth. Hudson's ass tightened, and that was enough. He erupted, gripping the sofa while his body shuddered with pleasure, pulsing into Luke's mouth.

"Sorry," he gasped afterwards. "I didn't want to come so soon."

Luke sat back and swallowed. "It doesn't mean that was your only chance."

He was right. Sweating, breathless, Hudson was far from done. "Stand up," he told Luke, slipping to the floor himself.

Luke kissed him first, pushing his tongue into Hudson's mouth to share the taste of cum. His fingers went to Hudson's hard nipples, squeezing and tugging. Hudson's cock hadn't had time to soften before he was rock hard again.

"Oh, man," he cried. "What are you doing to me?"

"Having a lot of fun."

As Luke rose to his feet, Hudson was already reaching for his belt buckle. He tore into his trousers, pulling them open. Luke wore a pair of black briefs with thick white lettering around the waist band. The outline of his cock bulged against the material, with a damp patch around the head. Hudson pulled his briefs down, releasing his cock. It hung heavily forward, slightly curving. Hudson was delighted to discover that he was uncut. Hudson had been circumcised as a child and found the foreskin of other men infinitely fascinating and arousing.

The pink head of Luke's cock protruded through the folds of skin. Hudson took it straight into his mouth, sucking, licking, exploring, but soon he was overcome by desire. He put both hands on Luke's thighs and moved his head back and forth. He lacked Luke's skill of deep-throating without gagging, but more than compensated with enthusiasm.

"Yes," Luke gasped, resting his fingers on Hudson's shoulder but doing nothing to control him or the pace.

Hudson recognised the tightening of Luke's breath, the tension throughout his body when he was close, and increased his effort until the hot fluid flooded his mouth. Luke came so much he had to swallow rapidly.

Luke's body curled over itself, bending at the waist to lean on Hudson. "Stop. Stop," he cried, still shuddering. "Oh, shit. That's too intense."

Hudson withdrew, licking his lips, enjoying the sight of Luke's flushed features.

Still naked, Hudson moved onto the sofa, flopping back, legs spread, hands over his head. "Whew. Man, that was good."

With his trousers around his knees, Luke shuffled over and dropped down bare-assed next to him. His chest heaved as he mirrored Hudson's position, but letting one hand rest on Hudson's thigh. Hudson hitched closer until their naked hips touched. For a few moments they said nothing. Hudson caught his breath, still relishing the afterglow of orgasm, and the taste of Luke that lingered in his mouth.

"You obviously don't remember, but we have met before," Luke said. "Before this week."

"Huh?" Hudson was not one of those guys who forget a man as soon as he's blown his load. He ran his hand along the back of the sofa and stroked Luke's head. His hair was slightly damp. "I'd remember you."

"No, no. Not like this. It was about three years ago. Do you remember doing a run in the play 2:22? I was in London visiting a mate and he dragged me to your press night. I wasn't covering the show for the *Chronicle*, but I tagged along anyway. The after party was packed and we were briefly introduced."

"I remember the play all right, even the press night. But I'm sorry. I really don't remember meeting you."

"There's no reason you should. We barely shook hands before the publicity guys whisked you off to speak to far more important people. I was one of about sixty in that room. But I remember you all right. Hudson Rhodes, the big American movie star."

Hudson laughed. "I think you're taking the piss now. That's what you say here, isn't it? Taking the piss."

"Indeed, we do. But I'm not. I was pretty knocked out in those few seconds. I've met big stars before and

I'm very rarely starstruck, but there was something about you that resonated. An indefinable charisma."

"Oh, come on. You really are taking the piss."

Luke laughed. "It's true."

"I'm not even famous. Not really. Especially not over here."

"Don't be so modest. I've seen you in loads of things. Not theatre, but TV. You've got a pretty impressive résumé of British film and drama these days."

Hudson shrugged. He had always found it embarrassing to talk about himself and his achievements. A trait he hadn't found in many other people in his profession. "I like working over here. I get more job offers here, too."

"Do you live here permanently these days?"

"No, New York. But I'm rarely there. My brother is staying in my place while I'm away. He might as well move in full-time."

"Especially if the play goes to London."

"We'll see."

He glanced at Luke's beautiful uncut cock. Even soft, it was mightily impressive, lying against his silky-smooth balls. His pubic hair was neatly trimmed above it. Hudson was pleased to note he hadn't completely shaved his pubes off like a lot of modern guys did.

"Maybe we should have dinner, before the food you brought spoils."

Luke turned and kissed him on the mouth. "Now that we've both had our appetisers."

Luke stood first, allowing Hudson to steal a glance at his fine ass. It was as hot as everything else about him. His cheeks were high and pert, the lower curve coated in a fine layer of dark hair. He hoped Luke would allow him to explore that much further sometime. Then he pulled up his pants, covering the gorgeous peach.

"Awww," Hudson complained dramatically. "That spoils it."

Luke flashed a look over his shoulder. "I thought you wanted to eat."

"I do. Your ass."

He laughed and picked up Hudson's jeans, tossing them playfully at him. "Maybe for dessert, eh?"

Hudson loved the way Luke watched him as he got dressed, his desire clear in every glance. They came together again to kiss and Hudson copped a feel of that fine ass before heading to the kitchen.

The apartment was too small for a proper dining table, so he set two places at the breakfast counter and refreshed their glasses.

"If I'd been more prepared, I would have cooked something myself," he said, getting the hot food from the oven.

"After everything else you've been through today, I don't think it's out of order to cheat. You like to cook?"

"Hmm." He brushed against Luke's back to reach the upper cupboard where the plates were kept. "That's why I chose this apartment rather than a hotel. I wanted a kitchen to cook in. There isn't really time during rehearsals but once the play is running, I plan to make all my own meals here. It's a nice way to relax before a show. Do you cook?"

"I can make pasta and stir through a jar of sauce, if that counts. I don't really have the time for much else, and when I do, it's never worth the effort it takes to shop, prepare and cook from scratch. Especially for one. I'm hopeless in the kitchen anyway."

They set about opening the cartons. The smells made Hudson's stomach rumble. If it only tasted half as good it would be fantastic. "Let me repay you for all of this by making you a meal one night. Something special."

"Deal," Luke said. "I'll even bring the condoms."

Hudson loved the way Luke laughed, with a huge smile that illuminated his otherwise serious face. Something inside Hudson flipped at the sight of it.

There was pasta with meatballs in an ultra-rich sauce, garlic bread, salad and a side dish of roasted peppers and red onions.

"This is delicious," Hudson said after the first mouthful. "You'll have to tell me where this place is."

"It's not that far from here. A five-minute walk. I usually dine in the restaurant, but knew they did takeaway food, which was ideal for tonight."

"You sound like an expert on the city. You'll have to give me some tips for places I can check out. I feel like I've barely scratched the surface."

"I'll show you around when you have the time."

Hudson tasted the tomato sauce. It was even richer than he'd imagined. "What else do you do for fun? Besides eating out and theatre."

"I think I've already told you. I spend what little time off I have at home. Just enjoying the beach, watching movies. I try to get to the gym two or three times a week."

"What kind of movies are you into? Art house stuff?"

"Well, yes, but only for work. When I'm relaxing, I like to watch pure trash. Escapist stuff, you know. Action, horror. That's why I was a bit starstruck that time I saw you in London."

"Because of the trash I've made?"

They chuckled together.

"That makes it sound worse than it is," Luke said. "I'm a bit of a horror movie buff. I especially love all the old stuff, especially slasher movies. Actually, one of your old movies is one of my favourites."

Hudson froze with the fork halfway to his mouth, his mouth suddenly dry. "Oh, yeah. Which one?"

"I doubt you remember much about it. It was so long ago. But it's called *Red Hills Massacre*. The one with Baby Face — the killer."

That motherfucking film. Hudson lost his appetite.

Chapter Nine

"Stay Out of Trouble"

Hudson waited until the Uber was right outside the building before exiting the lobby. The three photographers who were waiting on the doorstep started clicking their cameras before he'd even opened the door.

"Any news on Julian's murder?" one of them yelled.

"Who do you think did it?" another shouted.

"Will the play be cancelled?"

Assholes.

"Guys, just let me be. I've lost a friend. I've nothing further to say." He pushed past them and jumped into the back of the car.

"Do you think it's a copycat killer, Hudson?"

What the fuck does that mean? He pulled the door shut and locked it, keeping his head down to deny them a decent picture. "Just go, please," he told the driver.

One of the photographers had his camera right up to the window. It banged against the side of the car as the vehicle pulled away.

"What was that all about?" the driver asked.

"You don't want to know," Hudson said, sinking low in the back seat and breathing deeply.

The Vermont Hotel was on the waterfront, just across the river from the Concert Hall. He was relieved to see there were no press people waiting outside. Hudson thanked the driver and credited her with a tip, before hurrying inside.

The hotel foyer had high ceilings and marble tiles on the floor with lots of dark wood and brass railings. The concierge gave him directions to the lounge, where he found more white marble and lots of plush soft furnishing, all cream and gold velvet. In the corner of the large room, a pianist played a decent rendition of an old Bond theme.

"Over here, my darling."

Jo Peel was on her feet to greet him with open arms, a vison of big blonde hair, cleavage and statement jewellery. Unlike most showbiz people, Hudson was not into hugging and kissing, but Jo was not the woman to say no to. He allowed himself to be enveloped in her warm, sweet-smelling embrace. Once done with the hugs, she stood back, holding him at arm's length in a formidable grip to look him up and down.

"My God, you've been through it, haven't you? Have you slept at all?"

"Not much," he admitted, relieved when she released him and sat back down.

Jo was midway through one of those sparse breakfasts that only seemed to be served in posh hotels. Meagre portions of bacon, sausage, eggs and avocado spread across an oversized plate. "You need to eat something." Rings flashed on every finger as she cut a tiny piece off the end of a sausage and put it in her mouth before chewing daintily.

"I'm not hungry." There was already a pot of coffee on the table and a spare cup. He helped himself and dropped in a lump of brown sugar.

Jo patted her mouth with a napkin, careful not to smear her crimson lipstick. Despite her old-fashioned glamour-puss image, Hudson knew from experience that Jo was no pussycat. She drove an extremely hard deal and fought like a tiger for the rights of her clients. It was impossible to determine her age. The cosmetic enhancements and dramatic make-up made her appear young and old at the same time. Hudson guessed she was in her late forties but could be ten years off in either direction. His eyes were fixated on a huge sapphire and diamond pendant that hung just above her well-hoisted breasts.

"Aren't you worried you'll get mugged walking around with something like that?"

She rolled her eyes exaggeratedly. "I'll like to see someone try. They won't survive with their fingers intact, that I guarantee." She had a deep, raspy voice that had a two-packs-of-cigarettes-a-day quality, though Hudson had never seen her smoke in all the time he'd known her.

It was not yet eleven o'clock. Jo had flown to Blyham early that morning. "What time did you have to get up to start putting all this together?" he asked.

"This"—she ran her fingers over herself from head to waist—"was achieved in fifteen minutes in the back of the car to the airport. I might look high-maintenance, darling, but I could practically do this in my sleep."

He laughed. Despite the circumstances, it was good to see her. He no longer felt alone. "What time are Andie and Rav arriving?"

"They've been and gone."

His mouth dropped. "They've what?"

"It's fine, sweetie, don't worry. Everything is taken care of. They're getting it from all angles at the minute — police, investors, cast, crew, *their* goddamned agents. Even I felt a scrap of sympathy for them. It can't be easy."

"I don't understand. What do you mean? Everything is taken care of?"

"To use a showbiz cliché, the show will go on."

He let that digest. He'd more or less accepted that it would, though he had mixed emotions at the prospect of continuing. "How?" he said at last.

"Rehearsals have been stood down for the rest of the week. Enjoy the time off and try to get yourself together. There's a great-looking spa in this place. You should book yourself in and take advantage. Relax, unwind, recharge."

"What about the play? What about Julian?"

"I can deal with most things, but Julian's death is something I can't get involved in."

"Murder," he corrected. "Julian's murder."

"Murder, yes. It appears that way." She raised the cup and saucer and sipped. "I represented him for a couple of years myself. Back in his early days. I got him some good work in TV. He wouldn't have been playing understudies now if he'd stuck with me. No offence to you, my darling. Julian was a fine actor. He could have carried this play with ease."

"I know he was." After Luke had left last night, Hudson's mind had been in a state of turmoil. When he'd eventually gone to bed, he'd been unable to sleep and had watched an old episode of *Casualty* in which Julian had appeared as the victim of a road accident, who was trying to escape from a violent relationship. It had been a powerful performance that had Hudson in tears by the end, even more tragic given current circumstances. "So, what are they planning to do? Just replace him?" He clicked his fingers disdainfully. "Like that?"

"You know that's how it works. Everybody is replaceable."

"For fuck's sake."

"We don't have to like it, but it's the way it is." Jo's phone rang. She glanced at the screen without picking it up, bared her teeth, then rejected the call. She turned back to Hudson, fully composed. "Look, it's shit, I know it is. We both do. But there's a lot of money invested in this show. Two years of planning just to get to this stage. The goal has always been to make this a hit, take it to London and then on road. Potentially Broadway. Julian was a lovely man, but he was one small part of the production. It will go on without him. It must."

He nodded sullenly. "You're right. I don't have to like it."

"But you have to get that talented arse of yours on stage in two weeks' time and make this the smash we know it has to be."

"Jesus, two weeks. We're already behind."

"Rav and Andie have agreed to cancel the first three preview performances to allow you to make up for some of the lost rehearsal time. But opening night goes ahead as planned."

Hudson slumped further into his seat, thoroughly depressed. What she was telling him made complete sense. As a professional, he knew that. He'd replaced other actors at short notice, and been replaced himself a couple of times—it was all part of the business. The opening of any new show was always fraught with problems, but this was so much worse. "I don't know how we'll make it. It's too much."

She slapped her hand on the table, her rings clattering off the marble. "Get it together, Hudson. Look, you've got the rest of the week off. Do whatever you want to mourn Julian. Get drunk. Fuck your blues away. Do whatever you need to do, but make sure it's all out of your system and you're laser focused by Monday morning. You'll need to be to get this show running. It's going to be under more attention than ever when it opens."

"Jesus. As if we weren't stressed enough already."

"Yes, it's shit, but I don't make the rules. I just play by them. Everyone will be talking about *Darkest Blue* by the time you hit that stage. You need to be on your A-game." Now she picked up her phone and tapped her nails against the screen. Her mouth raised at the corners. "Well, I'll be damned."

He groaned. "If this is more bad news I don't want to know."

Jo licked her lips. "It's the silver lining. The show has sold out overnight. The complete four-week run."

"What?"

"Ticket sales were pretty good already for the first two weeks and weekends, but the whole run has been snapped up now. Restricted view and nosebleed seats, the lot. Wow." She grinned. "You realise this means a big step closer to the West End transfer."

"It's grotesque."

"You might want to check the socials, darling. Everyone is talking about you. You've gained several hundred thousand new followers on those accounts you don't even update. I'll get Nehal right on it. He can post some new content on your behalf and give all these new people something to engage with."

"No," he said, outraged. "I don't want to encourage it."

"You have to."

"I don't suppose Rav and Andie told you I've been receiving weirdo fan mail at the theatre? That's the reason I don't engage with strangers online. I have no fucking clue who any of them are."

"Even more reason to let Nehal run the accounts. You won't have to interact with any of them. It's a win–win, darling, take it." Jo began gathering her things together, stuffing everything into an oversized Chanel bag. "Now, I've got to make some calls. You know what you have to do, just relax for the rest of the week and be one hundred per cent on it for Monday."

He reached for his coffee, but it had gone cold. "Are you flying back to London?"

"Later tonight, but you can reach me by phone at any time, you know that. Day or night. In the meantime, I'll be fielding off offers of work for you. The phone has been going all morning at the office. Most of them want you to give an interview but there are some legit work offers in there too. Big ones. But until we have the dates for *Darkest Blue* in London, I can't commit you to much of anything."

If it wasn't all so distasteful, Hudson would admit a grudging respect for the way Jo was handling the situation. He sighed and got to his feet. He had no idea what he was going to do with himself these next few days. He'd been looking forward to the opportunity to explore Blyham and the local area, but the circumstances were not ideal.

"What about Julian's part? Will they find someone to take over before Monday?"

Jo did not look up from her phone.

When he repeated the question, and she looked at him sideways, he knew the answer. "Oh, for fuck's sake. Don't tell me, you've put up one of your other clients, haven't you?"

She shrugged. "They needed someone who could start at short notice, and I have the perfect person. I sent him the script last night and he's already learned his own role, he's working on your lines right now."

"You're unbelievable."

"He did a video audition with Rav and Andie first thing this morning and they've agreed that he's the best option. Let's face it, you need somebody who could start yesterday, and I've found the solution. Now, don't look at me like that, Hudson. I told you—I don't make the rules."

"You just know how to play them," he groaned.

"Exactly." She smiled. "Now, go on, get out from under my heels. Mama has work to do."

As Hudson was walking away, she called after him. "Hey."

"What now?"

Jo was on her feet, one hand on her hip. "Make sure you stay out of trouble between now and Monday. You'll be a lot harder to replace."

Chapter Ten

Bad News

Hudson hadn't quite got his head around the fact that one of Luke's favourites movies was *Red Hills Massacre*. The cheap piece-of-shit horror film he'd made more than twenty years ago. The same movie that was also popular with Robbie Wiseman, his British stalker. *What the fuck was that all about? How can anyone seriously be a fan of such crap?* Even so, he was happy when his phone rang on Friday afternoon and Luke's name flashed on the caller ID.

It had been a soulless twenty-four hours. Despite his best intention to get out and explore the city, he'd been holed up in the apartment since he'd left Jo at the hotel the day before. There were still a couple of photographers hanging around outside and his phone had been lighting up with calls and messages from people he hadn't talked to in years. Hudson had been in no mood to socialise.

Thankfully, there was a gym on the corner, and he'd been able to sneak out past the press guys in a hasty disguise and fit in a decent two-hour workout that morning. By the time he got back upstairs, showered, dressed and cooked himself a light lunch of tuna steak and couscous, he was feeling more affable. Luke's call came at just the right time.

"Hi," he said, genuinely pleased to hear from him. "How's it going?"

"Better now I'm speaking to you. More importantly, how are you doing?" That lovely accent was like fine whisky, having an instant, warming effect. Any uncertainties he'd had about Luke vanished at the sound of it.

"Meh. Not sure I even want to go there. But it's nice to hear from you."

"I guess you've had a lot to deal with."

"No shit. I take it you've heard the latest. That the show is going ahead."

"I did, though Sal Morte didn't strike me as an obvious replacement."

"Me neither." Hudson hadn't even been aware that his agent also represented the Spanish actor. He was a similar age to Hudson, so understudying him wouldn't be a problem in that respect. The fact that the character was American and Sal had a very heavy Spanish accent might be a bigger concern. But as Hudson had no intention of missing a performance—all Sal needed to worry about was nailing the small role he'd been cast for. "He's already arrived. Rav and Andie are going to work with him over the weekend before we resume on Monday."

"And how do you feel about that?"

"That's another tricky question I'm not sure I can answer just yet."

"Fair enough."

It really was good to talk to him again. They had ended things on such a strange note the other night when Hudson had freaked out about Luke's terrible taste in movies. It seemed even stranger now, but his head had been all over the place on Wednesday. Much of the day had been a blur that he struggled to remember with any clarity. Trying to look back on it was like watching one of his old films. He felt a distance and disconnect from it.

"Listen," Luke said. His voice had taken on a serious tone that Hudson was unused to. "I've got some news. It's not out in public, but my colleague has told me it's one hundred per cent legit. Are you free for a catch-up later this afternoon?"

"Sounds ominous."

"Hmm, I can't lie, it's not great. But, given the circumstances, I won't go into it over the phone. Do you want to get a drink somewhere after work and I'll fill you in face-to-face?"

"That would be tricky. I've still got the paps camped outside. Wherever I meet you, they're bound to follow."

"I could come by your apartment, like the other night."

"I'm getting sick of these four walls. Didn't you say you lived somewhere on the coast? How about I meet you there and we can go for a walk along the beach instead?"

"That's the best idea I've heard all day. Give your handlers the slip and I'll pick you up at the corner of Broad Street and Salvin Road just after five."

* * * *

It was a brilliantly clear and warm afternoon. Hudson changed into cream chino shorts and a light blue T-shirt before leaving the apartment. His moustache had gotten a little neglected, so he'd spent some time trimming and grooming. He'd started to become quite proud of the thing.

He was surprised to find that the photographers were no longer waiting on the doorstep, but hurried off anyway, in case they were only taking a break, though surely they knew by now that they would get nothing from him. In shades and a baseball cap, he snuck down the side alley and cut through to the main road.

Luke hadn't told him what kind of vehicle to expect. The glorious weather seemed to have triggered a mass early exodus from the city and the traffic moved at a sluggish pace.

Butterflies danced in his stomach as he waited at the kerb. When he'd gotten off the phone with Luke earlier, he'd been intrigued to know what his news would be, but as the time came closer, he'd been more excited about seeing Luke again. They'd ended the other night on a strange moment. Hudson was certain he would not allow that to happen again.

He'd been standing on the street a little over five minutes when a modest grey Peugeot tooted and pulled over to the kerb. Hudson rushed forward and leapt into the passage seat, as the driver behind issued their own blast of the horn in protest.

"Hey." Luke grinned at him sideways, easing back into the traffic lane. "Sorry, but I think I'll be lynched if I stop here."

"Just keep moving and do what you have to do," Hudson said. *Damn*, he looked good, in a short-sleeved, open-necked shirt and light grey trousers. "Have you been in the office all day?"

Luke nodded, checking the rear-view mirror. "I would have been observing your rehearsals, so it's given me a chance to catch up on some things I've been putting off."

Hudson pulled off the baseball cap and ruffled his hair. "Will you be joining us again next week?"

"I certainly hope so. Though it might be a little busy in there."

"What do you mean?"

"Your rehearsals. The podcasters start sitting in from Monday. Unless Rav has cancelled them, but I can't see him doing that now everyone is talking about the show."

Hudson glanced at him, confused. "What are you talking about? Podcasters?"

"Corman Curtis and Amber Payne from the *Beyond Blyham* podcast."

"What about them?"

"They'll be there next week?"

"Since when?"

Now Luke seemed perplexed. "Since always. I'm pretty sure it was arranged around the time my access was. They're going to put out two specials covering the last week of rehearsals and the lead-in to opening night. I thought you knew?"

"Motherfuckers," he muttered. "I'll kill Rav and Andie when I see them."

"Then they didn't tell you?"

"Just like they said nothing about you. If you hadn't told me the night before, I'd have been as clueless then, too. They're turning this into a fucking circus."

"They need publicity."

"Not anymore, they don't. There's isn't a spare seat to be had for the entire run." He clenched his fingers. He was getting angry again. None of this was Luke's fault. It was those two assholes running the production. "Sorry. I don't mean to take it out on you."

Luke took a left turn and the road in front of him was suddenly clear. He increased his speed. "I heard about the ticket sales. It's gruesome but hardly unexpected. People naturally have a morbid curiosity."

Hudson nodded solemnly. "I meant to say, I read your obituary on Julian. It was fantastic. Very thorough. Thanks for doing that."

"I'm just sorry I had to write it, but people deserve to be reminded of all the great things he did. It was even picked up by a couple of the national papers."

Luke stayed quiet a moment as he negotiated a tricky four-lane overpass and suddenly they were out of the city. The sea was visible on the horizon. Hudson hadn't appreciated how close Blyham was to the coast.

"Julian is the reason I wanted to speak to you," Luke said. He glanced sideways. "I've got some more information on the circumstances of his death."

"Do I want to hear it?"

"Probably not, but I think you should anyway."

Hudson tutted. "Come on then. Let's get it over with."

"I was speaking to a colleague on the crime desk this morning. He's been asked not to publicise the info he's been given. The cops don't want to sabotage an ongoing investigation, and for the sake of Julian's family. I didn't even make the connection myself. Not at first. Not until I saw the crime scene photographs."

"You saw those? Fuck. I don't want to see them."

"You can't. I was only shown them on a tablet. I don't have hard copies, but it was enough to freak me out."

A veil of dread and oppression swirled around Hudson's head. It seemed to push him down into the car seat. "What did you see?"

Luke paused, taking an audible breath. "You already knew he'd been stabbed, right? He'd been found in the alley, early on Wednesday morning."

"Sure. And?"

Another long pause. "From the pictures I saw this morning, Julian's body was arranged in a certain way. A very particular way. And it reminded me of something. Or rather someone."

"What are you talking about?"

"It reminded me of you. In particular, what happened to you in *Red Hills Massacre*. Julian was dressed in nothing but a pair of tight white underpants, exactly like you wore in the movie. His body appeared to be arranged in a pose that I'd swear mimics your death scene. The police still haven't found the rest of his clothes. There's no trace of them."

A strange floating sensation came over Hudson and it sounded for a moment like he was listening to Luke from underwater. "*Red Hills Massacre*," he managed to say at last, incredulous.

"It's too much of a coincidence," Luke said, "that your own co-star should be killed in a copycat of a film you starred in."

"It's no coincidence. Of all the fucking films." He noticed Luke was watching him. He cleared his throat. "I found out on Monday that someone has been sending all this bizarre mail to me, care of the theatre.

Rav didn't think I needed to know. He thought it would unsettle my performance."

"What kind of mail?"

"The *Red Hills Massacre* kind. More specifically, still images of that death scene, along with cryptic, bullshit messages."

"Where is all this stuff now? The letters and pictures."

"Rav has them. He was going to get someone to look into it."

"Fuck. He won't even know of the connection yet." Luke gripped the wheel. "I'll turn around at the next junction. We need to get back to the theatre and hand them over to the police. It can't be a coincidence."

Hudson swallowed. His throat was parched. "How far is it to your house?"

"We're nearly there. A few more minutes."

"Keep going. Please. I need a drink. I need…a few moments to get my head around this. I'll call Rav and Andie when we get there."

"Are you okay?"

"No. Keep driving please."

Luke drove onto a road that ran parallel to a wide, flat beach. There were a dozen or so cottages dotted along the waterfront, and he pulled onto the drive of one of the houses two-thirds of the way along. There was a small, immaculate garden behind a low stone wall. The prettiness of the place would have astounded Hudson if he wasn't so numb. He noted the details without taking them in.

"Come on," Luke said, getting out of the car.

Despite the low ceilings and small rooms, the interior of the house was surprisingly light, thanks to a patio door at the front. Luke took him through to the kitchen.

"I've got beer and wine, but you look like you could do with something a lot stronger." He opened the freezer compartment and pulled out a bottle of vodka. He put ice into a short tumbler and poured the spirit on top. "Do you want a mixer?"

Hudson shook his head and accepted the drink. He took half of it in a single mouthful. Thankfully it was smooth, with no burn in the throat.

Luke put a gentle hand on his shoulder. "Better?"

He nodded.

"You're as white as a ghost."

"I'm still processing." He investigated Luke's deep, dark eyes. "You're sure about Julian's body? You weren't just imposing your own ideas onto the images you saw? You did say you were a fan of that movie yourself."

"A hundred per cent sure. I could see the connection as soon as I saw the photo. Even if the killer hadn't made the effort to stage Julian's body in that exact position, the white underpants would have been more than a coincidence. Julian. You. The film. There's no way it's just a fluke."

No. Hudson had already guessed as much. And he already had a stalker who'd proved himself to be obsessed with *Red Hills Massacre*. His biggest nightmare had become a reality.

"We're better call the cops. There's someone they need to find. And quickly. Before he does it again."

Chapter Eleven

At the Beach House

Hudson's first impressions of Detective Sergent Benito Coppola were favourable. He arrived at Luke's house less than an hour after they'd made the call. He was a very attractive man in his mid-to-late thirties, his dark hair greying at the temples and deep lines adding character to an otherwise too handsome face. Despite the heat, he was well dressed in a navy pinstriped suit with a blue silk tie.

That was as good as it got. Within minutes of coming inside, he revealed himself to be an arrogant, narrow-minded prick.

"I don't know where you're getting your information from" — he shot Luke a withering glance as he spoke — "but we could do without amateur sleuthing hindering our investigation."

"I understood that anything relevant to the investigation was important," Hudson said.

"I'm not sure a twenty-year-old B-movie qualifies on that front." Coppola stood in the centre of the kitchen, taking it in with an owl-like one-eighty-degree turn of his head. "How come you're here? I thought you were staying in the city."

"I am, but I've been a prisoner in my apartment. Luke invited me over to clear my head."

The detective eyes swivelled back to Luke. "Did he now? And why is that?"

"What has that got to do with anything?" Luke asked.

Coppola shrugged. "I know what reporters are like. How far you're prepared to go for the sake of a story."

"I could say the same thing about cops," Luke shot back. "Or, in the case of Blyham police, how little they're prepared to do to reach an easy conclusion."

Hudson was shocked at how quickly the atmosphere had soured. "Do you want my statement or not?"

After a long beat, the detective nodded and pulled out a seat at the table.

"I'm going to shower and change," Luke said. "I'll leave you to it."

He had barely left the room when Coppola asked, "How well do you know him?"

"As well as anyone around here. We met through work."

His face was blank as he took out a pad of proforma sheets. "And he knew Julian King too?"

"Of course he did. He knows everyone involved in the play." Hudson topped up his vodka and sat down. "Do you two know each other? You and Luke? I'm sensing an atmosphere."

"I don't have a lot of time for journalists. But yes, I know him. Now, what's this all about?"

Coppola refused to confirm or deny what Luke had told him about the way Julian's body had been placed in the alley, but his brow furrowed with interest when Hudson used Luke's iPad to pull up a series of still images from the film, namely his death scene. Hudson went further and found a clip of the movie on YouTube. He passed the screen to DS Coppola. He had no interest in watching it ever again, as his character, dressed in nothing but skimpy white underwear, was stalked and murdered by the killer in a creepy baby mask.

"Actually, I have seen this film," Coppola said, sounding surprised before hitting replay on the clip. "God, I'd forgotten all about it. That mask scared the shit out of me. I had nightmares about it afterwards."

Hudson grimaced. Baby Face, as the killer had since been labelled by horror movie fans, was truly a fucked-up sight. The actor behind the mask, Steven Stone, was a pure sweetheart. Apart from some serious behind-the-scenes tensions with the director, the shoot had been unremarkable. Hudson had only been on set for three of the five weeks of production. It was everything that had happened afterwards, and how it had tainted his career, that left a sour taste. The Baby Face mask had become a staple of Halloween, and Hudson avoided social media even more than normal throughout October as his timeline became polluted with images of the movie killer.

When the clip finished a second time, Coppola put down the tablet.

"So, someone has been sending you mail relating to the movie?"

He nodded. "There's one guy in particular who is obsessed with the film. Robbie Wiseman. When I was previously over here, I had to take out a Stalking Prevention Order against him when his behaviour got out of hand. He used to send me letters and images related to the film all the time."

"And you think he's at it again?"

"It seems likely. I can't imagine there are too many people who are hung up on that old piece of shit."

"And you think it might be connected to Julian's death?"

"I have no idea. But from what Luke has told me about the way Julian's body was staged, it sounds like a huge coincidence."

Coppola tutted. "Your friend has a big mouth."

"You haven't denied that what he's told me is true, though."

Coppola ignored the remark. "Where is this fella Robbie Wiseman now?"

"Again, I have no idea."

"Did Julian receive any of these weird letters?"

"I don't think so. When I told him about them, he never mentioned it." Hudson took a drink. "But Julian wasn't in that film, so why would he?"

"And why would anyone who is a fan of the film think it was a good idea to kill him and stage it to look like your death scene? You realise how insane all of this sounds?"

"Of course I do, but surely it's worth your time to look into it. Just in case the two things are connected."

The detective rattled his pen on the tabletop. "Where are all these letters you received? Do you have them?"

"No. They're with Rav Millard, the producer. He was going to see if he could find out where they came from."

Coppola shook his head. "Another amateur sleuth," he muttered. "All right, I'll look into it. But first I need to take all of this down in a statement." He pulled the pad in front of him and clicked on his pen. "Let's go through this all again from the beginning."

It took over an hour for Coppola to write down everything that Hudson told him. Luke came back down in baggy shorts and T-shirt, with wet hair. When he realised they were still busy, he grabbed a beer and disappeared into another room. Hudson watched with envy, wishing he could be with him rather than with this obtrusive police officer.

When Coppola finished his paperwork, Hudson called Rav and told him to get all the letters and photographs together and someone from the police department would call to collect them. Rav sounded distracted and pissed off and didn't stay on the call for long. Hudson didn't think it was the best time to bring up the subject of the podcasters Rav had arranged to join the already-fraught rehearsals from next week. That argument could keep for another day.

Finally, the detective was done. "We'll start by tracing the whereabouts of this guy Robbie Wiseman. You're sure the stalking order is still in place?"

"I checked with my lawyer. It was made indefinitely, and I haven't applied to have it revoked, so yes."

"Then it should be straightforward enough." He gathered his things together. "Are you staying here now?" There was a sly quality to the question.

"For a few hours, yes. Then I'll be back in the city. But you can reach me on my cell wherever I am."

It was a relief when he finally left. Hudson couldn't put his finger on it, but there just seemed like there was something very off about the guy.

Good-looking shit.

He found Luke sitting in the front garden, enjoying the evening sun as the detective drove away. He looked stunning with the low, golden rays reflecting on his light brown skin. He'd kicked off his shoes and his bare, toned legs were stretched out in front of him.

"All good?" Luke asked.

"I think so. He's written down all the details, though I'm not sure how seriously he's actually taking it. Strange guy."

"Yep, I've always thought so too."

"I got the impression you two have history."

Luke laughed. "Not in the way you're thinking. Benito is one of the few openly gay officers in the Blyham force, not that you would ever know it. He's done very little to support the community. All through the Blyham Strangler months, he kept his head down to avoid any of the controversy. People were pissed at the police back then. Rightly so. Their efforts to protect the local men who were being targeted were negligent. Even now that the Strangler is behind bars, hate crime is still raging all over the city. Not just homophobia, but racism, anti-Semitism, disability abuse, transphobia. They have weaponised the word woke and use it as blanket term to attack anything they don't like. I'm not saying that's Benito's responsibility—just because he's gay, he doesn't owe us something extra—I just think he could do better. A hell of a lot better. But he's not the only gay cop on the force I know, and they're all as career-focused as he is."

Hudson took the chair beside him, raising his face towards the sun, which was still warm. He drew the fresh sea air deep into this chest and sighed.

"Do you feel better for reporting it?" Luke asked.

"Hard to say. I'd rather none of this was happening, but the more the cops know, the quicker they can find Robbie. Or whoever else is behind all this." He inhaled again and ran his hands across his face, trying to draw away the tension. "This is an incredible place you have here."

"Isn't it? I couldn't believe my luck when it came on the market. The previous owners were an elderly couple who had to sell up when they moved into sheltered accommodation. It was very old-fashioned when I bought it. But over a few years, one room at a time, I've gotten the house just how I want it." He sipped his drink. "Thankfully, I managed to hang onto it after the divorce. Kris hated living out here. He hated the house too."

"How long were you married?"

Luke gave a long sigh. "Less than two years, but we were separated for more than half of that time. It's the timeless story of someone turning out to be a completely different person on the other side of the ceremony." He finished his drink. "Feel like a walk along the beach? It's good for clearing the head."

"Brilliant idea."

Luke locked the front door, and they headed across the road and down to the beach. The sand was soft. Hudson took off his shoes and the walk was instantly easier. Luke did the same and they strolled to the water's edge, before turning right.

"It's beautiful," Hudson said, taking in the long, flat shoreline.

"Mmm. North and south of here, the coast becomes more rugged and rocky, but we're in an even plane here."

"I really need to get out and explore this area more."

"There's plenty to see," Luke said. "You can go up the coast further into Northumberland, or south, to Yorkshire. There really is no bad way to go. I'd be happy to show you around."

Hudson grinned. "I'd love that."

A light breeze ruffled his hair. He admired the way it caused Luke's T-shirt to ripple over his body, skimming his chest, revealing the hard peaks of his nipples.

What's happening here? He couldn't deny he was attracted to Luke and with every moment they spent together, he found himself being drawn closer to him. He had a magnetism that was irresistible. What was holding him back? Everything that was happening. He had enough complications already without the hurdle of a new relationship. And how far could that relationship go anyway? He was only going to be here for a few more weeks. Who knew when they would be able to see each other after that.

Hudson would be flying back to the States once this run of *Darkest Blue* was done. He had the secondary lead role in an indie movie coming up. Unless the play transferred to the West End, he didn't have any pending commitments in the UK to keep him here.

"This was supposed to clear your mind," Luke said.

"Sorry?"

"The walk. It was supposed to cleanse you of all your worries. Your face tells a different story. You look more distracted than ever."

"Sorry," he said again, attempting to shake his reservations off. Why worry about something that was weeks away? Shouldn't he embrace life now? He was lucky to have that opportunity. Julian surely didn't.

They paused a moment to look out to sea. The water was remarkably calm. He'd always heard that the North Sea was one of the roughest in the world. There was a wind farm in the distance. Farther out, he spotted a tanker and some other kind of vessel, heading northwards.

"Is that a cruise ship?"

Luke shielded his eyes from the sun. "Looks like one. It will be heading to the terminal on the Tyne."

The cold water rushed around his ankles. "It really is amazing out here. I've always loved the idea of living by the ocean, but I'm a city boy at heart."

"There are plenty of cities close by. Blyham, Newcastle, Sunderland, Durham. They are all within less than an hour drive from here. It's possible to have the best of both worlds."

"You're proof of that."

When they returned to the house, a petite tortoise shell cat was sunning itself on Luke's garden chair. It gave a small tweep and rolled onto its back and stretched at the sight of him. Luke grinned, stroking the cat's chin and cheek.

"Is this your cat?"

"I'm one of her minions," he replied. "This is Molly. She lives at number three but makes herself at home in every house on the street."

Molly wriggled around on her back, kicking her legs and purring loudly.

"That's one lucky cat," Hudson said.

Luke looked at him, grinning. "Pussies aren't the only things I know how to spoil."

Hudson laughed loudly. "I'm very happy to hear that."

Luke picked up the cat and sat down, placing her on his knee. She rearranged herself so he could stroke her head. She looked like she was smiling. Hudson took the chair beside him. Suddenly Luke was serious. "Listen, I know things are weird right now. Fuck, that's putting it mildly to say the least. And you've got a lot going on, but I just want you to know that I'm glad you're here. I'd glad you trust me."

"I'm glad too," he said, meaning it. "It's hard to believe that on Monday night I was so pissed at the idea of you coming to the studio. And you've turned out to be the one ray of normality in this batshit crazy week. I appreciate that so much. I appreciate you." Hudson's face grew warm as he spoke. He was probably blushing, and he didn't care. He meant it.

Who else would have supported him in all this madness. Not Rav or Andie. Or Jo. They each had their own interests to look out for. He had only made a serious personal connection with two people while he'd been in Blyham.

One of them was dead.

The other was sitting right beside him.

Whatever reservations he might have, surely this was the time for him to seize the moment.

Chapter Twelve

Early Evening Heat

Once the sun left the front of the house, the temperature dropped. Molly leapt from Luke's lap, stretched, and sauntered off in search of somewhere warmer.

"I think that's our cue to move inside too," Luke said.

The purpose of coming to the beach had been to help Hudson relax, and in the last hour he had achieved that. It was surprising how calming it could be chilling with a hot guy and a cute cat.

Hudson was pleased to note that Luke had locked the front door behind them. He hadn't wanted to spoil the mood by mentioning it, but on the wacky chance that Julian's killer was obsessed with *Red Hills Massacre*, they couldn't afford to be complacent. It continued to rile him that the stupid old movie occupied so much space in his head. He refused to allow it to spoil anything else today.

They slipped off their shoes at the door and he followed Luke into the kitchen, admiring the firm flex of his butt cheeks at he walked.

"Hungry?" Luke asked.

He realised it was after eight. "Actually, I'm not. Not yet anyway."

"Me neither. Beer then." Luke reached into the fridge. He produced and uncapped two bottles. "Cheers," he said, handing one to Hudson.

"Cheers." They clinked bottle necks.

The kitchen was small but stylish, with buttermilk-coloured units, black granite counters and dark oak flooring.

"You did all this?" Hudson gestured around the room with the bottle.

"It was all my idea, but I didn't do the physical work. I'm a writer, not a joiner. This was the last part of the house to be renovated. The most expensive, too. I had to save up a while before I could afford it."

"But worth the wait to get exactly what you wanted."

"Exactly. Want to see the rest of the house?"

"I'd love to. Lead the way."

Off the kitchen was a small patio area, with outdoor dining table and chairs, and views of fields and moorland behind. "The outlook can't compete with the front, but I like it. It's more private, too. No traffic passing in this direction."

"It's stunning." The nearest properties to the rear were nothing more than tiny boxes of colour on the distant landscape. "Don't you ever feel isolated out here?"

"Not at all. I'm just a few miles from the city. There's even a pub in walking distance if I want to get out without taking the car."

Upstairs there was a very small bathroom, with a shower over the tub.

"The one drawback of living in a small house. There was no way to expand on the bathroom without losing another room, but it's a sacrifice I was prepared to make."

Next was a compact study, with barely room for a desk and chair. The desk was piled high with books on art, theatre and history.

"That reminds me. I ordered your book about the Empire Theatre. It arrived yesterday."

Luke's mouth popped open. "You did?"

"I'm afraid to say I haven't had concentration to do more than flick through it so far."

"Hardly surprising. I would have given you a copy if I'd known you were interested."

"No chance. I don't want freebies. I want to support local talent."

"Very noble of you."

Luke's thigh brushed against Hudson's as they stepped back into the hall, sending a frisson of excitement all through his body.

There was a small bedroom at the rear of the house, with unspoiled views of the fields behind. "Guest room," Luke explained. "Not that I do a lot of entertaining here."

"You already mentioned that before. You like time by yourself on your days off."

He grinned. "Well remembered."

The main bedroom was the largest of the upstairs rooms. The first thing to impress was the wide window with a clear view of the sea beyond. The evening sky was still a spectacular shade of blue. The floor was the same dark oak as the kitchen, with a colourful rug in front of the window. The large double bed was dressed with immaculate cream covers and pillowcases.

"This is like a luxury Airbnb," Hudson said. "Are you sure you really live here?"

Luke laughed. "I forgot to mention I'm also a tidy freak. Never leave the house each morning without making the bed and clearing away the clutter."

"You don't strike me as a clutter kind of person."

"And you'd be right."

In the shadowy light of the room, with his strong nose and chiselled cheekbones, Luke looked like a matinee idol from Hollywood's golden era. Hudson's pulse, which had already been running fast, quickened further. He swallowed. "I've just realised where you've led me to."

"Ah, and I thought my plan was watertight."

"I guess it is. It worked, didn't it?"

Luke's eyes glistened. "It did. There's something else." He stepped around Hudson, his groin brushing against his butt as he did. He slid open the top drawer of the bedside cabinet. "I've been shopping." He reached inside and produced a box of condoms.

Hudson flushed with relief, delight and pure pleasure. He pulled his wallet from his pocket and opened it. "So have I." Inside was a strip of four condoms.

They stared at each other. Lips wide, their eyes full of hunger, they pounced across the room. Hudson grabbed Luke's head in both hands, fixing his mouth on top of his. Luke's hands went around his body, one hand gripping his shoulder, the other resting on the curve of his spine. They kissed deeply, pushing their tongues against each other's.

Hudson moaned as Luke ground his hardness onto him. There was no mistaking his intent.

Then Luke's hands were under Hudson's T-shirt, pulling it over his chest. They broke from the kiss just long enough for Luke to haul the garment over Hudson's head and cast it to the floor. Hudson shuddered when Luke's hands caressed bare skin. He'd been longing to be touched like this ever since that first time on Wednesday night.

"God, you're gorgeous," Luke said, pressing kisses along the side of his jaw.

Hudson gripped him, savouring his body, the heat, the smell, every part of him. He tugged at Luke's shirt, pulling upwards until it was free. They pressed their bodies together, bare skin against skin. Hudson moved his mouth along Luke's neck, down to his shoulder, tasting him.

Luke matched Hudson's hunger, beat for beat, pulling at his belt and fly to release his shorts. Hudson lifted his hips, wriggling until they were clear of his ass, and kicked them off the end of the bed.

"You've done it again," he said between kisses."

"What's that?" Luke murmured.

"I'm completely naked and you're not."

Luke's hands wandered across his torso, going down, gripping his cock. "Yes, you are. I like you this way." He tightened his hold, taking Hudson's balls and the base of his dick in a firm grasp. Hudson was wearing his black leather strap. "Do you wear this all the time?"

"Only when I want to feel good."

"Oh, you *definitely* feel good," Luke said, squeezing him tighter.

Hudson grabbed at Luke's belt, unfastening the buckle, tearing into his shorts. He shoved them over his ass, releasing him and getting off his underwear too. Luke squirmed until he was free and shoved them to the floor with Hudson's.

"Better?" he asked.

"A hundred per cent."

They pressed their naked bodies together, writhing and thrusting their hard cocks. Hudson's abdomen was soon moist with the slick of their shared pre-cum.

"I want to fuck you," Luke whispered as they fell onto the bed.

It wasn't something they had discussed in any great depth—their preferred positions for sex. It didn't matter. Hudson wanted him and would take him anyway that he could. He spread his thighs wide, arching his back to offer himself. "Have me," he said. "Have all of me."

Luke climbed on top of him, getting between his open legs. He slid his fingers into his crack, locating his hot opening, gently stroking and teasing. "I've been thinking about this since Wednesday night. Despite everything else that's happened, I haven't been able to get you out of my mind."

He reached across to the bedside drawers and grabbed a bottle of lube to go with the condoms. Luke put a condom on first, before dribbling lube onto his fingers and returning them to Hudson's ass. Hudson shivered with delight as the cool liquid made contact with his hole. Luke eased a cautious finger into him.

"Tell me if I'm going too far. If I hurt you."

Hudson hooked his arms around the backs of his knees, rolling them into his chest to show Luke just how eager he was. "Don't worry about me. I like it rough."

Luke's dark eyes widened as he squirmed another finger into him. "Is that a fact?" He slipped back and forth, opening Hudson's tight passage.

"As rough as it gets."

Luke poured more lube into his palm and covered his dick, before moving into position between Hudson's thighs. Hudson rolled his hips even higher, bringing them into perfect alignment. He needed this. He needed Luke, more than he had on Wednesday, when they'd both been numb with shock. He wanted to feel the fullness of this beautiful man inside him, to feel their two bodies united.

Luke pushed the head of his cock into the opening, then leaned over, pressing his mouth against Hudson's, kissing him all the while as he thrust inside. The stretch was intense as Hudson opened. For a few seconds it seemed impossible that he would be able to take him. He'd overestimated his abilities. It had been too long since he'd been fucked. He couldn't do it.

And then there was release as Luke pushed through his body's natural resistance. They groaned, their tongues thrusting. Luke's balls nudged against his upturned ass, filling him completely.

Hudson had what he wanted. He let go of his legs and wrapped them around Luke's waist, drawing him closer, deeper.

"Yes," he groaned. "Now fuck me good."

Luke ground into him, kissing, plunging further. In no time, their skin was wet with sweat, their bellies sliding together. Hudson arched his back, relishing the sensation of being so utterly full.

"Let me turn around," he gasped after a while. "Take me from behind."

Luke pulled out, leaving him temporarily empty. Hudson scrambled onto all fours and pushed his butt at Luke. Luke shoved back into him and grabbed his waist in both hands. Soon his lean hips clapped against Hudson's ass.

Hudson had almost forgotten how great it was to surrender his body completely to another man. He dropped his head and shoulders to the bed and raised his ass. "Harder," he demanded. "Fuck me harder."

Luke jabbed into him with hard, staccato thrusts.

"Like this?" Luke hissed.

"Yes. Yes. Fucking destroy me."

He would never have believed until he came into this room that he would let his guard down completely, especially to a man he'd been opposed to just a few days earlier.

Luke wrapped his arms around Hudson, pulling him upright. With his chest pressed against Hudson's back, he buried his face in the crook of his neck. Hudson reached backwards, seizing Luke's hips and pulling him tighter against his buttocks, wanting all of him inside.

Hudson's hair was plastered to his face. His eyes stung with sweat. This was what he'd been missing for too long—being dominated, being ridden for someone's else pleasure.

They changed position again and again. Hudson wanted to experience Luke and his big cock in every way he could. Best of all was when Luke rolled him onto his back and grabbed his ankles, holding his legs high and wide, and pounded him. The angle brought his cock in perfect alignment with Hudson's prostate. Hudson put his hands behind his head to avoid the temptation of touching himself. His pleasure was already at a heightened peak. The slightest extra stimulus would tip him over. He gazed at Luke as they fucked. His handsome face was flushed dark with passion. He bared his teeth and gasped with every thrust.

"Can't hold on much longer," Luke said.

"Come inside me," Hudson pleaded. "Let me have it."

Luke's cries became louder and more desperate sounding. Hudson watched him carefully, wanting to time it so they came together. When Luke appeared like he could take no more, Hudson gripped his own cock. The explosions started instantly. A profound feeling deep in his balls that pulsed all through his groin, heightened by the tight strap. Delaying, prolonging the intense pleasure, until finally he spurted, one intense pulse of pure ecstasy after another, spewing white-hot cum across his belly.

They collapsed in a shuddering heap. Luke fell across Hudson. Their bodies were on fire. Their hearts hammered against their ribcages.

"Holy shit," Hudson cried, gasping for air.

Luke lay helplessly on top of him. Hudson wrapped his legs around his waist again, reluctant to release him, despite being so utterly satisfied.

Luke eventually pushed up onto his elbows. His face, right above Hudson's, seemed more beautiful than ever in the low evening light of the room.

"That was fucking hot," Hudson said at last.

Luke kissed him on the mouth. "It sure was. I can't remember when I last felt so in tune with anyone."

Once they had cleaned up and disposed of the condom, they lay naked on top of the bed, above the covers. The warmth of the day lingered in the bedroom. Through the open window came the sound of the sea against the beach, the distant squawk of gulls. Hudson lay beside Luke, his right leg draped across his thigh, his arm flung carefully across his chest.

"Want to spend the night?" Luke asked.

"If that's all right with you." Now that he was here, Hudson had no wish to return to the city. Blyham was becoming oppressive, stifling. Although they were only a few miles away, everything seemed much freer, more welcoming out here.

Less dangerous.

Luke ran his hand along the backs of Hudson's shoulders.

"It's more than all right. I can't think of a better way to spend a Friday night than with you."

"What about Saturday morning?"

"Well, I've always said the nicest part of going to bed with a man is waking up next to him."

Chapter Thirteen

Night into Morning

By eleven o'clock there was still a hint of daylight in the night sky. Hudson would not have been aware of the fact if he'd been in the city. Even from his balcony, the urban light pollution would have spoiled the sight, but from Luke's living room, with the patio doors wide open to the elements, he had the perfect opportunity to take it all in. They sat together on the sofa, their bare feet propped on a solid wood coffee table, drinking and enjoying the chilled-out mood.

Luke had made a light tuna Niçoise for dinner, cobbled together from the refrigerator, and they'd spent the rest of the evening just where they were. Hudson could still make out the gentle white caps of waves rippling the surface of the sea just a hundred yards away.

"Doesn't it ever flood?" he asked. A slight promenade on the other side of the road was all that stood between the sea and the house.

"Not in the time I've been here. It was a worry when I first moved in, but even at high tide, the water doesn't come anywhere close to the road. I guess it's something to do with the local geography or seabed that I don't understand."

The house was small, but Hudson had to admit that what it lacked in size was more than compensated for by the spectacular locations and views.

"Do you plan to stay here long?" he asked.

"As long as I'm working in the area, I can't see any reason to move. I would hate to go back into the city. I used to live near to where you're staying now when I first came to Blyham. It was ideal at first. Close to work, to the theatre and galleries. I was younger then, and more eager to go out on the gay scene too. The novelty soon wore off all those things."

"I get that. I used to be the same. Wherever I went, I wanted to check out the gay scenes, hit the bars and clubs, meet local guys. I've barely seen anything since I got here."

"I could say it's not as good a scene as it used to be, but that's probably more to do with me. The bars haven't changed much in the time I've lived here. It didn't used to be as violent as it is now. I'm not sure how safe I'd feel in the gay triangle at night these days. Especially on my own. I was talking to a guy at work, just a couple of weeks ago, who was followed by a group of guys in a car, taunting him and hurling insults. He had to take shelter in a late-night coffee shop until they got bored and moved on."

"Assholes."

"Absolutely. Sadly, there are a lot of them about."

"Have you always been out to your family?"

"Not always, no. For a long time, in my late teens and early twenties, I wasn't even out to myself. I found it a struggle. My parents were a dream. They've always been open-minded and liberal in their thinking, but it took me a long time to accept myself. I was at uni when I had my first boyfriend."

"I'm sorry to hear that. Not about your parents, about your self-doubts."

Luke laughed. "Oh, I had a lot going on as a teenager. My sexuality was a small problem next to everything else. Racism, bullying. The place we lived when I was growing up was not the most tolerant. It was only when I went to university in Manchester that I could relax and finally be myself."

Hudson stroked his bare thigh. It was good to have Luke open up to him like this. He wanted to know so much more about him. "What did you study?"

"Literature and journalism."

"I thought you might have said drama. Given how much you love theatre."

"I do love theatre, but the last thing I want to do is get up on a stage." He shuddered. "All those people watching. All that expectation. It fills me with horror. I always wanted to be a writer, so that's the path I followed."

"And something you'll stick with?"

"Mmm. As long as I can. I'd like to branch out into other kinds of writing besides journalism. I'd love to do another book. I just haven't latched onto a suitable subject yet. I'd even like to write a novel one day. How about you? Has your career panned out the way you wanted?"

Hudson laughed. "Fuck no. I mean, I'm doing all right now and love the opportunities I've been given to work on the stage, especially in Europe, but I can't say my career has gone the way I envisaged."

Luke shifted to look at him more directly. "How come? You had quite a few leading man parts in your twenties. Rom coms and such. Would you like to have continued that?"

Hudson squirmed slightly. "Those were not the happiest days of my career. Sure, I'd love to get those lead roles again in big budget movies, but not at the expense of my sanity." He noticed the curious look on Luke's face and continued. "To play those romantic leads, shit, even to play in those shitty horror films, I had to master two roles. The character in the movie and the role of straight leading man."

"Oh," Luke said. "I get it."

"People say things have changed for the better, but they used to say that back then too. Sure, there are more openly queer actors working today, but how many of them are getting mainstream work, let alone playing straight leads? Maybe two. The rest are just as closeted as I had to be."

"What made you decide to come out?"

"I didn't decide at all. I was outed. And as soon as I was, the offers of work vanished." He blew an imaginary puff of smoke. "Just like that. Overnight, I was nobody."

"Shit," Luke said. "I didn't know it was so bad. To be honest, I'm more familiar with your theatre work than movies. Obviously, I remember you from *Red Hills Massacre* too."

Hudson groaned. "Can we not talk about that shit again. Please."

"Sorry."

"It was a huge fucking hit. Number one at the American box office for two weeks, but I don't want to be remembered as the dude who got chopped up with an axe by a killer in a baby mask. All while wearing a pair of underpants." He sighed. "I wish I'd never accepted the damn part. Especially now."

Luke squeezed his thigh. "Sorry, again. I shouldn't have mentioned it. Let's not spoil what's been a bloody amazing night because of it. How about a nightcap? Something to calm the nerves."

"That sounds perfect."

Luke stood and stretched. His body looked extraordinary, seen from behind, with the doors open to the night in front of him. If Hudson was a director and shooting a movie right now, that was an image he'd use in the film and the trailer. Hell, it was good enough to put on the poster. Luke collected the empty glasses and headed to the kitchen.

Hudson inhaled the clean sea air and sank deeper in the sofa. The tension that had built over these last few days would probably never ease, but spending time with Luke this evening, enjoying his company and his beautiful house, had gone a long way towards making him feel better.

* * * *

Sunlight flooded the bedroom early the next morning. Hudson woke around five-thirty with Luke spooning into his back, his hard cock pressing against his ass. He rolled over into his arms and the sex that followed was spontaneous and passionate. Afterwards they fell into a light sleep, their arms around each other.

The peace was broken by a loud knocking at the front door.

"What?" Luke grumbled, pushing onto his elbows.

"What time is it?" Hudson asked, shielding his eyes against the light.

Luke checked his watch on the bedside table. "Seven-thirty. Who the hell does that on a Saturday morning?"

More heavy banging at the door.

"It sounds like someone is trying to break in," Hudson said.

"I'll break something when I find out who it is." Luke swung his legs off the bed and stood. He pulled on last night's shorts without underwear and lunged out of the room, still half asleep and unsteady. When the knocking came again, he yelled, "Hold on. I'm coming."

It sounded to Hudson like someone was beating in the door with their fists. It gave him an instant bad feeling. He got out of bed and pulled on his own shorts, crossing to the window.

There was an unfamiliar car on the drive, parked at an awkward angle, as though the driver had just slewed in from the main road. Leaning forward, he could just make out the head and shoulders of a man at the door. He had a dark blond crew cut which was heavily receded at the front. Hudson didn't recognise him.

Luke opened the door.

"Good fucking night, was it?" The man's voice carried clearly up to the bedroom. He took a few steps backwards, bouncing from foot to foot. His face, all the way up into the hairline, was puce.

"What are you doing here?" Luke said. Though his voice was quieter than the blond guy's, his anger was just as clear.

"You're fucking actors now, are you? Rich and famous. The likes of me aren't good enough for you?"

Shit. Who is this asshole? Luke had told him more than once that he was single, so who was this prick pulling the angry boyfriend act?

"I don't need to guess who told you," Luke said. "But it's neither his business nor yours. Get back in your car and get stuffed, Kris."

Kris swept his arms around, his chest held out. Hudson could see the flare of his nostrils from above. "Benito is a mate. He cares about me. Not like you."

Benito? The cop. What does he have to do with this?

"You've been drinking, haven't you?"

Kris grimaced. "That's all you ever say. Of course I haven't been drinking. It's not even eight o'clock."

"Then you had a real skinful last night. You reek of booze. You shouldn't be driving in this state."

"I'm in a state because of you." He jabbed his finger at Luke. "You. I notice you're not denying anything. So, how long have you been fucking him?"

This has to be the ex-husband. Jesus. No wonder the marriage didn't last.

Hudson wondered if he should go down. He wanted to back Luke up but knew nothing about this situation. Perhaps the sight of him might tip Kris completely over the edge. The man looked like he was on the verge of losing it already.

When Luke spoke again, his voice was calm. "You don't have any claim over me, Kris. I don't know how many times, or how many ways, I have to tell you that. We've been finished for a long time."

"You'll never be rid of me. That's what marriage means. You'll come back to me — we both know it. Why'd you have to spoil it by fucking that bastard Yank?"

"I'm not going to argue with you anymore. You don't know the situation and you don't want me to call the police."

"For what?" he yelled. "Visiting my husband in my own fucking house?"

Hudson wondered if he should call the cops himself. This guy was so wound up he was a danger to Luke.

"I'm not your husband and this is not your house." Luke's voice was astonishingly composed. The more irate Kris became, the calmer Luke was. "Now go away, and don't come back. I don't want to see you again."

"He's still in there, isn't he?" Kris looked at the bedroom window and locked eyes with Hudson. The redness in his face seemed to deepen. "He's there. You bastard whore. He's up there." He waved his fist at Luke.

Hudson had heard enough. This asshole was going to hurt Luke if he wasn't stopped. He hurried for the stairs.

"Kris, this is your last warning. You've got one minute to get in your car and get off my drive. If you're still there, then I'm calling the police and I'm telling them everything."

Luke closed the door as Hudson reached the bottom step. He put his full weight against it and turned the lock. Outside, Kris continued to shout, but any sense he might have made was lost inside his rage.

Luke's ear was pressed against the door. They held their breath, listening.

At last, there was the roar of an engine and grinding of gears. Hudson moved to the front window and watched as the car tore off along the seafront road.

Luke was still pressed against the door. Hudson put his arms around him from behind and felt his entire body shaking.

There was nothing he could say.

Hudson hugged him silently and tried to reassure him.

Chapter Fourteen

Divorce and Opportunities

"He's a cop?"

"Yep," Luke said. "Just about hanging onto the job, but yes, he's a copper."

They had returned to bed. It had just gone eight o'clock. Hudson lay on his back with Luke's head resting on his shoulder, his arm draped across his chest. Luke hadn't spoken for several minutes after Kris had left. He'd gone to the kitchen and drank a glass of water, before taking Hudson's hand and leading him back upstairs. This was a wholly different side of Luke than he had seen before. Vulnerable, lacking in confidence. Whatever had happened between those two men in the past, the scars ran deep.

The curtains stirred with a light sea breeze, but the room was warm. They had pulled a sheet to their waists, leaving their chests exposed.

"I take it he wasn't always like that."

"Not at all. When we first got together, he was funny and light-hearted. A real cheeky chappy sort who could always make me laugh. I met him when I was covering a story. Environmental campaigners staged a protest at a gallery in the city. They threw cans of tomato soup over several of the art works. Kris was one of the first police officers at the scene and I interviewed him for the paper afterwards. He was so charming, with these blue twinkling eyes. I was quite bowled over."

Hudson ran a reassuring hand along Luke's arm. He waited for him to continue, not wanting to force the story out of him if he didn't want to tell it. Seagulls squawked in the distance.

"It was great in the beginning. I've never met anyone quite like him. He even came to the theatre with me and pretended to be interested when he was clearly bored out of his mind. I should have realised then how easy it was for him to become someone he wasn't when it suited him. He proposed on my birthday. We went on a trip to London, saw a matinee in the afternoon, then went for dinner at a restaurant in The Shard. He got on his knee and asked the question in front of all the other diners."

Making it almost impossible for you to refuse. Hudson kept the thought to himself.

Luke stretched and rolled onto his back, staring at the ceiling. His hands were clasped over his abdomen. "It seemed like he changed the moment the ceremony was over. We went to Barcelona for our honeymoon, and he started an argument on the plane with a group of lads who were on a stag party. I managed to calm him down before it got out of hand. I seriously thought we were going to be arrested when we landed. It put him in a foul mood for the rest of the day and I ended up eating alone that first night of the trip. Great start, eh?"

"Was he drunk?"

"Pissed as a fart. He told me he was nervous about flying and I bought it. I must have been blind with love because all the signs that he was a secret drinker were there from the start. I stupidly thought he was one of those men who get drunk on just one or two beers, without picking up on the fact that he would knock off a couple of shots each time he went to the bar. But that was really just the honeymoon period. Once we settled into normal life, he made little effort to hide it from me. He would start drinking after breakfast on his days off. Hit the vodka as soon as his shift was over when he was working."

Hudson rolled onto his side to look at him. His put his hand on top of Luke's. "That can't have been easy."

He sighed. "I told myself he had a high-pressured job. He needed the booze to relax. If I ever mentioned it, he'd say all the cops on the force were drinkers, and he didn't have a problem. It's pathetic really, the things we're prepared to believe."

"It's natural. He was your husband. Of course you were going to support him."

"I stopped inviting him to the events I was attending because I knew he'd get drunk and embarrass me."

"Again, not your fault."

He frowned. "I'm certain I could have done more to help him, to get him support in those early days, but I'd already begun to pull away. And that only made things worse. Kris became jealous and controlling. Every day was a barrage of questions—where was I going? Who would be there? Why did I stay so late? And he was angry all the time. I couldn't do anything to please him."

"Is that what brought things to an end?"

He shook his head. "No. I might even still be married to the arsehole if things hadn't reached a head in the way they did. I was having a drink and some food with a colleague before we went to review a new show. Kris wasn't invited. He was supposed to be working anyway. But he turned up at the restaurant and made a huge scene. Accused us of having an affair. Which was ludicrous. Dean was straight and had a new girlfriend each time I spoke to him. We managed to get Kris outside, before we were thrown out, but he just became more and more irate. Nothing I could say would calm him down. Then he punched Dean right in the face."

"Shit."

"Exactly. That was the final straw. It made me see sense at last."

"Did he ever hit you?"

"No. It was more of an emotional violence that he used against me. But I couldn't take any more. He fought against the divorce with all he had. The only reason he eventually went along with it was because Dean agreed not to press charges against him. It would have been the end of Kris' career in the police and that's all he really has. None of his family speak to him. Another red flag I missed at the start."

"So, what was that about this morning?"

"He might have signed the divorce papers but, as far as he's concerned, it's a temporary arrangement. For whatever reason, he thinks we'll get back together eventually. I don't know why. I haven't given him a single hint that could be a possibility."

"I heard you say he smelled of drink earlier. That's still a problem?"

"It appears so. He might have been telling the truth, and it was a residual stink from last night, but he'd still be well over the limit to drive. I should have called it in. Though, with buddies like Benito on the force, it's questionable how far that would go."

"Benito told him about us?"

"How else did he know you were here?"

"The fucker."

"Right. I wouldn't trust Benito Coppola as far as I could throw him. Just because he's gay, it doesn't mean he's on our team. Or even one of the good guys."

"From what you've told me, Kris is a functioning alcoholic. Why would Benito stick up for him?"

"Who knows? Maybe he thinks like I did, that Kris will change and sober up one day. I'll tell you one thing—it's put me off the idea of marriage for a long time."

They both laughed.

"What about you?" Luke asked. "Any ex-husbands I should be worried about?"

"No, I'm clear on that front. I just have run-of-the-mill nutcase stalkers. There's no marriage baggage attached."

"Ever been tempted?"

"I came close once," Hudson admitted. He drew his fingers up the line on Luke's torso, from his navel to his chest, before running them through his chest hair. "His name was Pete. A lawyer back in New York. He was a great guy. No major asshole issues. He was funny and intelligent and had a great job. He wasn't jealous or demanding. Didn't make an issue when work took me away for weeks at a time."

"He sounds perfect. What went wrong?"

Hudson shook his head. "It's hard to explain. It was kind of perfect on a surface level, but there was just something missing. We both got cold feet and realised we weren't the people we wanted to spend the rest of our lives with. We're still friends. Pete has got a partner now who does seem truly perfect for him. He's found that something that was missing when the two of us were together."

Luke turned on his side, so they were face to face. He put a hand on Hudson's hip.

"This is nice," he said. "I wasn't expecting we would share all this so soon. If my angry ex hadn't turned up, maybe we wouldn't have. But I'm glad we are. I feel like I know you better each day."

Hudson smiled and leaned in for a kiss. "I do too. And given how crazy this week has been so far, it feels kind of fitting that we're not obeying any of the traditional rules of dating."

Luke pulled his body closer, pressing their chests and bellies together. "Let's see what else we can discover."

* * * *

Hudson got back to his apartment around five. After the rude awaking from Kris, he'd spent a wonderfully relaxing day with Luke, talking, laughing, getting to know each other better. And fucking. There had been a lot of fucking. One of the highlights had been taking a long bath together. Though the house was small and the bathroom tiny, they had luxuriated in the hot water and bubbles for over an hour.

Hudson would have stayed much longer, but Jo had scheduled a video call with him at six and he wanted to take the call on his laptop rather than his phone. It was also so peaceful at the beach house that he didn't want to spoil it by mixing work with pleasure.

"You do realise it's Saturday evening," he said when his agent came on the call.

"Yes, and I'll be going out soon."

He noticed she was hosting the call from her bedroom. In the background, a little black dress hung on a door, while she appeared to be sitting at a vanity mirror in a white towelled robe.

"Couldn't it wait, then?"

Jo tutted. "Only losers wait, Hudson. Winners take the deals when they're offered, whatever the day or time. This is a twenty-four-hour business.

"What's so important that it couldn't wait until Monday?"

"You are," she said, pointing a long-nailed finger at the screen. "My phone has been blowing up for two days now with offers for you. Now, I know you said you didn't want to do interviews and are concentrating on the play, but I think you should hear some of the deals that have come forward for you."

"Unless it's a juicy acting job that's available after the play, you might as well save your breath. I've got enough to think about."

"The play comes first, of course it does. We all want that, but we're talking about some big fee offers for barely any effort."

Jo was a typical agent. Always hustling for the next buck. She fought hard for her clients and strove to get the best deal, but money was all that ever mattered.

"What are we talking about?" he asked wearily.

"I can get you on TV for an interview tomorrow. BBC Sunday Morning Live. It's mainly about politics and shit but they want you for a current affairs section."

"No."

She pursed her lips. "I thought you'd say that." She wrote something on a page off screen. "I don't suppose you're any keener on a sit-down interview with one of the national papers?"

"You suppose correctly."

She let out a long breath. "This would do great things for the play, you know."

"It's already sold out. Don't need it."

"Keep your eyes on the bigger prize, darling. London. West End."

"If that happens, it should be on the strength of the play and our performances. Not by exploiting a friend's death. Is this really what you've called me for on a Saturday night? To dangle a few trashy interviews?"

"None of this is small stuff, darling. These offers weren't there this time last week. You should take advantage. Think of what you could do with the money."

He ignored the remark. "Is there anything serious on the table?"

"*Celebrity MasterChef, Strictly* — that's just an expression of interest, not a certainty. *Celebrity Gogglebox, Masked Singer, Bake Off* —"

"You can stop there. I've heard enough. Are there any *acting* offers?"

"Possibly, but nothing certain. Would you be interested in doing a soap?"

"It would depend on the show and the part. And the length of the commitment. Six months max, nothing longer."

At last, a smile. "Well, that's something. Leave it with me, I might have good news by Monday."

"You're working all weekend?"

She gave a dramatic sigh. "Darling, I'm always working. Even tonight, I'm going to a party, but I'm hoping to seal a magazine spread for another client. Oh, if you're interested in doing one of those, I can get you some very nice money for it. Shoot in a luxury hotel, you can keep the designer clothes. You name it, I can get it."

Hudson shook his head with a smile. "I'm not interested. Good night, Jo. Try turning off for a while and enjoying yourself. Life is short, you know."

"And so are moments of opportunity like this. Think on everything I've said. I'll email you some details. You might change your mind when you read them."

Her email arrived in the next minute. Hudson laughed. She must have had it ready to send before she spoke to him. He shut down the laptop without opening it. Jo might not require time off, but he did. It would have been nice to spend longer with Luke, but he really needed to recharge his batteries ready for Monday. He also didn't fancy a run-in with Luke's alcoholic ex-husband any time soon. As much as he loved drama, that was one he would rather not play a leading role in.

Hudson realised he was still wearing yesterday's clothes. He bundled them into the laundry basket and changed into fresh shorts and a loose shirt. The hot weather continued, and the apartment didn't have air conditioning. He opened the balcony doors to get a breeze through and checked the refrigerator to see what he could have for dinner. Chicken breast, salad. After looking in the cupboards he realised he had everything he needed to make Southern-fried chicken. Perfect for a quiet night in front of the TV. He took the chicken out of the fridge to take the chill off it and poured a glass of wine. He'd have five minutes with his thoughts before he got to work on it.

He took the wine onto the balcony.

Thank God the reporters had abandoned their stake-out of the building, and he could unwind without fear of being photographed.

The sounds of Saturday night in the city drifted up from below. Traffic, laughter, music, people out to enjoy themselves. They had no care for the cloud that hung over Hudson and the production of *Darkest Blue*. Why should they? Life continued everywhere around him.

He sipped the wine and leaned against the balcony, breathing deeply. The air up here was clearer than down below, but it could not compare with being out at the beach.

As he focused on his breathing and tried to centre himself, he noticed a figure on the pavement, looking straight up at his apartment. Shit, he must have been wrong about the reporters. One lone wolf had decided to stick it out.

He squinted for a better view. There was something familiar about the figure.

A balding head. Rotund, middle-aged body. The upturned face stared directly at him.

Suddenly Hudson froze.

The man below was Robbie Wiseman.

His stalker was in Blyham after all.

And worse than that — Robbie knew where he lived.

Chapter Fifteen

Beyond Blyham

Instead of starting the week refreshed and prepared for a whole new round of rehearsals, on Monday morning Hudson was tired and ragged. On Saturday, he'd been up until almost two dealing with Blyham police officers who had taken three hours to come to the apartment and get his statement about Robbie Wiseman. The constables who had attended treated him like a crank, barely disguising their lack of interest. They had left with a vague suggestion that they would look at the local CCTV footage. Hudson had no hope they would follow through on that and intended to contact DS Benito Coppola in the morning.

After that, sleep had seemed near impossible. When he did at last fall off, it was a troubled and restless night. Sunday had not been much better. He'd attempted to focus on the script, but found himself constantly drawn back to the balcony, staring into the street, looking for his stalker. He'd become restless, not wanting to go out, but feeling trapped inside the apartment.

He could have called Luke, knowing he would be there in heartbeat, but something had held him back. As great as the last few days had been, their relationship was advancing at an accelerated rate. Hudson had always been wary about rushing into things and this was no exception. He trusted that his instincts about Luke were right, but he needed time and space to sit with them. To process what he was feeling.

When Luke sent him a text late in the afternoon to ask how he was doing, he lied and told him everything was great.

Sunday into Monday had been another restless night.

To make things worse, the walk from the apartment to the rehearsal studio that he enjoyed so much was out of the question. With everything that had happened and Robbie Wiseman in Blyham, he got a taxi across the river to the concert hall.

"Morning," Jax greeted him cheerfully at the stage door.

"Hi, Jax," he said, mustering enthusiasm he did not feel. "Any post today?"

Her eyes glanced over her shoulder and along the corridor. "Rav already asked me if there was any mail for you." Her voice was hushed. "I assumed you'd want to receive it yourself."

"Good work. You're right. I do."

She handed over a small pile of letters, containing an envelope with one of the all too familiar printed labels. Robbie Wiseman was nothing if not consistent. He thanked Jax and headed to the coffee shop.

While his order was being prepared, he opened the large envelope first, being careful not to handle it too much. It wouldn't make any difference. Robbie wouldn't have left any prints on the package. He'd been at his creepy practice for so long, he was practically a professional. Inside was a standard eight-by-ten glossy photograph. The surprise this time was that it was not a shot from *Red Hills Massacre*.

It was an image from a screen test he'd filmed for *The Leopard*, a superhero movie he'd been cast in many years ago, before being fired in the early stages of production. If it had gone ahead, the movie would have taken his career into the stratosphere. When the director was replaced, Hudson hadn't fitted with the new director's vision for the character and that had been the end of his hopes for mega stardom. In time, Hudson realised he'd dodged a bullet. *The Leopard* had gone on to become a multi-movie franchise with crossovers into other comic book films. Given how negative his experiences of fame had been at his current level, he didn't want that level of exposure.

His screen test and the costume and make-up tests he'd completed had been locked tight for many years, before eventually finding their way online.

The photo in the envelope showed him shirtless, obviously. His body was bigger, more ripped than he'd ever been before or since. Robbie's interest in him must be broadening. It made a change from seeing himself playing dead in a pair of white underpants.

Hudson called DS Coppola, who agreed to follow up on the call he'd put in over the weekend and send someone over to collect the latest letter. He sounded marginally more interested than his colleagues who had taken the initial report. Hudson wondered if he would pass the information on to Luke's ex Kris.

His mood fell further when he walked into the rehearsal room and spotted two newcomers, setting up recording equipment at the side of the stage. A man and a woman, both around thirty. *Shit.* He'd forgotten about the fucking podcasters.

The woman stopped what she was doing when she noticed he had arrived. The man, picking up on her interest, straightened and turned in his direction.

"Hi," they said in cheery unison.

"Fuck you," he muttered under his breath and ignored them.

Undeterred, they headed straight in his direction.

"Hey, Hudson, it's great to meet you." The man thrust his hand forward in an overfamiliar bro manner.

Hudson raised his hands to show that they were both full, one with a coffee cup, the other with mail.

Not to be put off, the man smacked him on the shoulder. "Corman Curtis, man."

"I'm Amber Payne." The woman curled her shoulder-length blonde hair behind an ear and fixed him full-on with her laser-sharp blue eyes. She looked like a perfect, filtered influencer profile image brought to life. "We're honoured to be here. It's really exciting for *Beyond Blyham* to be part of your amazing show."

"We're big fans," Corman said. Once again, his words were full of bro friendliness and devoid of sincerity. Corman was the Ken to Amber's Barbie. Gym-built physique, black hair, ultra-sharp lines in his facial hair. His jeans and T-shirt seemed like they had been tailored to his powerful body.

"Look," Hudson said. "I'll be honest with you from the start. We've got a shit load of pressure and stress upon us already. The last thing we need is to be a sideshow on your podcast."

"We're not like other podcasters," Corman said. The perfect smile did not falter.

"And, although we feature local issues, our show is listened to internationally." Amber was all business. "Our streaming numbers are consistently on the rise, month on month. We've won awards for…"

Hudson stopped listening to her. He knew exactly what they hoped covering the production of a play that was also the subject of an active murder investigation would do for their numbers.

He raised his pile of envelopes to stop them. "I'm sure that's all very impressive, but I'm not going to lie. If I had my way, you wouldn't be here. And I'm going to do my best to make sure you're here for the shortest time possible. In the meantime, I intend to stay out of your way. Please do the same for me."

With a smile as insincere as Corman's, he walked away.

"You've got the wrong idea about us," Amber said. "We'll prove our worth to you and you'll come around."

There wasn't a hint of uncertainty in her voice. This pair were not used to being turned down and rejection had little meaning for them.

"What's rattled your cage?" Steve asked. He sat on the floor, legs crossed as he stretched. For once, he was not posting selfies or inspirational messages on his socials.

"What do you think? They have no business being here."

Steve wrapped an arm around the opposite elbow. "I think they're pretty cool. And they're telling the truth. They do have a big following. Like, seriously massive."

"Excuse me if I don't shit myself with excitement over that."

Steve stared blankly at Hudson, as if he'd just spoken an entirely new language. And then, after the cogs had ground in his brain, he said, "Probably too modern for you anyway. I forgot you're from the dark ages."

Cheeky motherfucker.

Rav was on his phone when Hudson approached him. Without a care for his privacy, Hudson took the seat beside him and slapped the large envelope on the desk. He sipped his coffee while he waited for him to finish the call. There was nothing sinister in the other letters. Standard fan mail and requests for autographs.

"Another one?" Rav asked when he was done.

"Yep."

"I'll have my team look at it."

"No need. The police are on their way to collect it."

"Police? Oh right, they took the letters from last week too."

"Yes. Police. My stalker is here, in Blyham. I saw him outside my building over the weekend. These photos are coming from him. I'm sure of it."

"Are you all right?"

"Not really. I wasn't in the best of places when I came in." He pointed at Corman and Amber, huddled across the room. "And they are only making it worse. How long are they here for?"

Rav shifted his ass uncomfortably. "The next two weeks. They'll be here all the way to opening night."

Hudson's jaw dropped. "You've got to be kidding."

"Do you know how much media interest there is in this production now? We have to give them something. At least this way we can control what gets out. Corman and Amber are highly influential. It's not just their podcast, they've got TikTok, Instagram. Their reach is huge."

"I don't give a shit about their reach. This is...fucking heartless, is what it is. We've lost a vital member of our team, and you want to use that for...what? Some fucking online content?"

"That's not what this is about. We need them. The show needs them. Tickets don't sell by themselves, you know. And as great as you are, your name alone can't fill the theatre every night."

Hudson tightened his fists. "What the hell are you taking about? It's already sold out."

"In Blyham. We've got to focus on London now. I've got a shit load of interested investors, but they're not ready to part with their money just yet. The first week here and the reactions to it will get us over the line."

"And you don't think your cast and crew are talented enough to achieve that? You need cheap gimmicks. I thought this was serious theatre, not a return of vaudeville. Besides, we've already got Luke covering the build-up."

"It's a different world now, Hudson. And a whole lot of different mediums. We've got to be across the lot. We need to exploit every opportunity that's available to us."

Before rage threatened to consume him, Hudson took a deep breath in and counted to five, then exhaled once more on five. "I have nothing more to say other than that I'm disgusted that you see Julian's murder as an opportunity to exploit."

"C'mon, that's not what I said."

Hudson grabbed his coffee and stood. "Just keep that pair of assholes away from me. And while you're at it, do me another favour and stay the fuck away from me yourself."

* * * *

Sal Morte, Julian's hastily arranged replacement, arrived just before ten, accompanied by Manuella, who clung to his arm like he was her personal property. Hudson held back a few minutes as Andie and Rav made a fuss of the newcomer, greeting him like a saviour.

Hudson knew he had to cut the guy some slack. He'd been plunged into a situation beyond his control. None of this was his fault.

When things settled down, he went over to introduce himself.

"Hi, Sal, it's nice to meet you."

The Spanish actor shook his hand with great enthusiasm. He was around the same age as Hudson, dark-skinned and handsome with remarkable blue eyes. His salt-and-pepper hair was enviously thick. "It's an honour to be here, despite the tragic circumstances. I only want to do my best to serve your show and the man who went before me."

There was a beautifully soft lilt to his accent. Though his demeanour was confident, Hudson detected the notes of uncertainty in his expression. It would be impossible to hold a grudge against Sal, even if he wanted to.

"You'll be terrific. I'm sure of it."

"I already know Julian's role by heart. And I've been working all weekend on learning the understudy lines. I won't let you down."

"Don't put any pressure on yourself about that." Hudson held back from telling him that he had never missed a show in his life. Who wanted to tempt fate anyway? Given the troubled state of the production already, it would be Hudson's bad luck to break his leg and miss the whole damn run.

For the benefit of Sal, and the morale of all concerned, Andie decided they would spend the morning going over Act One. It was a great idea. After a few days off, it gave Hudson and his co-stars a chance to settle back into the rhythm of the script. Sal nailed his lines, bringing nuance and humour to the small part. Hudson's chest tightened with sadness as he realised just how easily the producers had replaced poor Julian.

Corman and Amber watched from the side, their eyes sharp and intent. He did his best to ignore them and was glad to see that Luke kept out of their way, making his own notes and observations from a subtle distance. Incredible to think that this time last week, Luke had been his antagonist, and now his presence was a comfort.

Though everything went well, it was a relief to break for lunch and to get some time with Luke. They found a table at the back of the coffee shop downstairs. Luke leaned straight in for a kiss, which Hudson accepted willingly, without a care for who might be watching.

"It's good to see you," Hudson said.

Luke's hand lingered on Hudson's waist until they sat. "I missed you yesterday."

His heart brightened at the news. "Really? I thought you had lots of work to do."

He shrugged. "I can still miss you, even when I'm busy."

Hudson flushed. If he was honest with himself, he'd missed Luke too. He'd gained absolutely nothing by spending his Sunday alone, other than becoming moody and melancholy. The answer to his troubles had been one call away. He'd been too stubborn to realise it.

No more pig-headedness.

He put his hand on top of Luke's. "What are you doing later?"

Chapter Sixteen

The Past Catches Up

By the end of the day, Hudson was exhausted, but not in the way he'd imagined. After his initial reservations about the podcasters and the argument with Rav, he'd put all the bullshit aside and focused on nothing but the story they were trying to tell. The rest of the cast also seemed to share his newly found dedication to getting it right. They were now working in honour of Julian, and they would continue the play in his memory. Even Steve had been less cocky and had shown a degree of respect.

Luke had to go back to his office for a couple of hours and they made arrangements to meet up around eight-thirty for a late dinner at nine. The whole world seemed off kilter, but for today at least, most things had gone right.

Hudson had trouble arranging a car via the app and decided to head outside to see if he could get a lift from the taxi rank along the road. As he exited the stage door, he was glad to see there were no reporters about. Things had also seemed to settle down on that front. No doubt it would ramp up again when they got closer to opening night.

He walked towards the front of the building.

"Hudson, hey. Wait up."

He didn't recognise the voice at first, but as he turned and saw the two podcasters hurrying behind him, his spirits sank.

Amber was in front, while Corman trailed behind, laden down with a large backpack and holdall of equipment. "That was awesome," Amber said, catching up with him. "You smashed that today."

"Absolutely," Corman said, drawing level. "I got goosebumps just watching from the side. That was, like, stupendous."

What kind of podcast do this pair run? They spoke like a couple of airheaded stoners.

"Thank you. It's been a hell of a day. I just want to get home and relax."

"Sure thing. We would, too, if we'd just been through all that."

"I was exhausted just watching you." Corman grinned.

Surely their eternal cheerfulness was the most exhausting aspect of their career.

"I'll see you tomorrow," he said, turning away.

Amber moved in front, blocking his path. Her expression shifted from joy to an approximation of solemnity. Hudson was getting a good idea of the dynamics of their podcast, and he had no desire to discover more.

"We got off on the wrong foot this morning," she said.

Now Corman formed an impassable obstruction in front of him. "Yeah. We don't want you to get the wrong idea about us." He put both hands across his heart. "We're totally sincere."

Hudson resisted the urge to laugh. "Look, guys. I appreciate that you're just doing a job. I was angry this morning and apologise if I spoke out of turn. But the truth is, I have a lot on my plate, and I don't need this kind of distraction. I meant what I said. I'm going to stay out of your way and appreciate you doing the same for me."

"But we really want to talk to you," Amber said. "I don't think you realise what a big deal this opportunity is for us. Not just sitting in on *Darkest Blue*, that's awesome enough, but getting to meet you."

"We're big fans. Huge." Corman grinned.

Hudson's defences prickled. He was not going to like what came next.

"The biggest," Amber added.

"We love you."

"We really do."

Hudson took a step back from them.

"Straight up," Corman continued. "We've been fans for years. We bought tickets for the play as soon as you were announced to be playing the lead. Isn't that right?"

"We absolutely did. We couldn't believe Hudson Rhodes was coming to Blyham."

"If you listen to episode two-hundred and seventeen of *Beyond Blyham*, you'll hear us talk all about it and how hyped we were by the news."

"It was really inappropriate, to be honest." Amber giggled.

Hudson looked at her quizzically.

"We were doing a deep dive into the Blyham Cat Killer at the time. Very serious stuff, but we just had to share the awesome news about the play with our listeners."

"We were hoping you would come on the show," Corman said. "To talk about the play obviously, but we want to go further than that. We want to talk about you and your career."

"All those great roles you've played," Amber gushed.

"We've seen them all. We know everything about you. Ask us anything, we'll know the answer."

Hudson raised both hands. "Guys, enough. That's never going to happen. If you do indeed know anything about me, then you'd know that I don't give interviews about myself. I haven't in years."

"If you listened to our show and find out what we're all about, you'll change your mind." Corman's smile looked larger than his face.

"I can assure you, I absolutely won't. Now, please, I have to go. I've got things to do."

"You know my favourite movie is *Red Hills Massacre*," Corman said. "Of all time."

"Mine too," Amber added with childlike glee.

Fuck my life. And that damned movie. Why is everyone I meet so obsessed with it? It was turning into a cult.

"I especially don't like talking about that one. In fact, I hate it."

Corman seemed astonished. "No way. That movie is a stone-cold classic."

"The best horror film of the last twenty-five years," Amber added. "Bar none."

Hudson laughed. This pair were ridiculous.

"And it was the first time you worked with Singer Fry," Corman said.

Hudson prickled further. "It was the only time I worked with him."

"What about *The Leopard*? You worked together on that too, right?"

Hudson's annoyance took a darker turn. "*The Leopard?* Did you two send me that picture this morning?"

They exchanged glances. Their inane smiles lost some enthusiasm.

"Er, what picture?" Amber said.

"We haven't sent you anything."

Were they lying? Was this jolly fan routine all an act? "The mail I've been receiving each day. Are you behind it?"

Corman's bottom lip fluttered like a grounded fish.

"Why would we send you mail?" Amber asked. "We knew we were going to be working with you anyway. We'll be seeing you every day."

"You mean, like, old-fashioned mail? Like, letters and stuff?" Corman laughed. "I don't know when I last posted a letter. Not even a Christmas card. Who even does that?"

He couldn't decide whether he believed their naïveté or not. It was some coincidence that they should arrive on the very day he received an image relating to *The Leopard*. What would they have to gain by provoking him with stupid mail anyway? Trying to unsettle him in the hope he would confide in them? Come on their podcast?

But no, it couldn't be them. Robbie Wiseman was behind the photographs. He had to be. He had form for that kind of behaviour and Hudson knew he was in Blyham. He'd seen him outside his building just the other night. He was on the wrong track suspecting Corman and Amber.

And yet, he didn't trust them one bit. What kind of podcast did they put out anyway? It was time he found out before he had any further interaction with them.

"We love *The Leopard*," Amber continued, as though his objection had not been raised. "But it would have been so cool if you'd actually got to star in it. Singer Fry directing and Hudson Rhodes in the lead. That's the film I really want to see."

"Absolutely," Corman said. "Did you actually shoot any footage with Singer before leaving the project?"

"As you seem to be better informed than me, I think you know the answer to that question. And now, for the third time today — stay out of my way."

He walked straight between them and away before they could block him again. His breath came fast and shallow. If there was one film experience that had been worse than *Red Hills*, it was *The Leopard*. At least the horror film had been completed and released. While *The Leopard* had indeed come out and become a huge hit, it had not starred Hudson.

Why had it come back to haunt him today, after all these years?

His experience in Blyham was getting stranger day by day.

When he got back to the apartment, he would take a hot bath to relax and listen to an episode of Corman and Amber's podcast to get a flavour of what they were really like. What was the tone and content of the show? The more he thought about them, the less he bought into their sweet, chummy routine. They had an agenda. To protect himself, he needed to figure out exactly what it was.

Hudson had reached the waterfront when he realised he'd got so preoccupied with the podcasters, he was walking in the wrong direction to get a taxi. Should he turn around, or keep going? He was practically upon the bridge. It would take him another five minutes to double back. *Oh, what the hell.* He would keep on going. It was a fine night, and if he kept powering through, he would soon reach the gay triangle and be home.

It wasn't even six-thirty and there were plenty of people out on the streets. If it was after dark, then things might have been different. He wouldn't have taken the risk. But what harm could there be at this moment?

He continued onwards, his thoughts returning to Corman and Amber. He'd have to keep his wits around those two. They had only been on the production for one day and had managed to unsettle him. He couldn't afford that. There was too much at risk. He'd have another go at Rav in the morning. Maybe he could convince him that their presence was detrimental to the show. Perhaps he could even convert some of the other actors to his side.

It was worth a try, and better than doing nothing.

He crossed the bridge to the other side of the city. It was great to be out in the open after spending the day holed up in a rehearsal studio. And yesterday he'd been confined to the apartment. He couldn't continue like this. He needed fresh air and space.

At least he had dinner with Luke to look forward to later. Nothing too fancy. Hopefully somewhere laid-back and relaxing. Maybe tomorrow night they could go back to The Blue Pearl. He hadn't been there since the night they first met. Live music and good food might be exactly what he needed, especially now the press wasn't following him around.

In no time at all he reached the bottom of Salvin Road, and the path steepened on the route into the gay village. He was almost there and feeling exhilarated after the negative exit from the concert hall. His emotions were all over the place. Up one moment and way down the next. *Darkest Blue* was turning into the most stressful experience of his entire career. And he'd played in his fair share of jinxed productions before now.

He waited for a gap in the traffic to cross the road. As he reached the other side, he caught sight of sudden movement behind him. A figure, dressed in T-shirt and jeans, darted into a doorway, too fast for him to take much in, but odd enough to trigger a reaction. He paused, waiting. Was it someone in a genuine hurry? Trying to catch a store before it closed for the night?

Or was it, as he suspected, someone who didn't want him to see them?

His pulse quickened while uneasy fingers skittered down his spine.

Years in the public eye had given him an instinct for when something wasn't right, and this didn't feel right at all.

Get a grip of yourself and get moving.

He was on a busy main road with lots of traffic about. People were still heading home from work while others were coming into the city for all the evening attractions. A bus went by that was packed with commuters.

Hudson continued on his way, quickening the pace. He was understandably jumpy, but there was nothing for him to worry about.

After another twenty yards, he whipped around suddenly.

The figure behind did not have time to react.

Robbie Wiseman. Even from the distance there was no doubt. The balding grey hair, the stout figure. Robbie came to a halt, realising he'd been seen. He glanced around, considering his options.

Hudson was torn between the choice of confronting him and getting the fuck away.

If Robbie was responsible for killing Julian, there was no telling what he would do now. He could be carrying a knife or a gun.

Hudson's survival instinct kicked in and he broke into a run.

He still didn't know this area well enough, and the apartment was a good five minutes away. Where the hell was he going to go?

When he risked a look over his shoulder, he saw Robbie in pursuit.

Whatever he decided, he'd have to make a decision fast.

Hudson kept running.

Chapter Seventeen

Hollywood Stories

There was nobody in the street ahead of him. No one to run to for help.

Robbie was too close for Hudson to pull out his phone and call the cops.

Time was running out.

He needed an escape right now.

There was a pub on the edge of the gay village. Julie's. He hadn't been inside. Didn't know much about it. He just prayed it was already open. Surely by this time of evening it should be.

Hudson put on a greater burst of speed.

So, Robbie was in Blyham. No doubt about it now. Had he been here last weekend when Julian was killed? It seemed almost certain.

The man was a maniac. Capable of anything. Hudson was sure of that now.

Hudson looked behind again. Robbie was gaining. For an older man, seemingly out of shape, he could really move.

Hudson had almost reached the pub. He sprinted harder.

Relief washed over him when he realised the front door was open.

He burst inside.

A young woman behind the bar jerked with surprise. Three middle-aged guys, sitting together, turned to look at him. Hudson stumbled into the middle of the room, gasping for breath. He bent over, his hands on his thighs, unable to speak.

Two of the men stood up and approached.

"Are you all right, fella?"

Hudson huffed, struggling to find his voice.

"Don't…" he panted, pointing at the door. "Don't let him in."

The bartender came out from behind the counter and went straight to the door, checking outside. One of the two men followed her.

"You best come and have a seat," the second man said, leading him to a table.

Hudson realised for the first time how badly he was shaking.

The man said his name was Dan. He sat beside Hudson while he caught his breath.

"Who was it?" Dan asked. "Another queer basher? This whole area has become a hellhole."

The bartender and the first man returned.

"Was it the stocky, balding guy?" she asked.

Hudson nodded.

"He legged it over the road and went down Broad Street. I think you're okay."

Her name was Kat. She got him a glass of water while he reported the incident to the police. Luke arrived before the cops did, rushing into the bar, his cheeks flushed. He ran straight for Hudson and put his arms around him.

"Are you all right?"

Hudson clung to him. Taking comfort from the strength of his body, the smell of his hair and cologne.

"I'm fine," he said. He'd gotten himself together by then. In some way he was actually relieved. When he'd seen Robbie on Saturday night it had been from a distance. He couldn't be one hundred per cent sure that it was him. But now there was no doubt. Robbie was in Blyham. It all tied into the sinister mail and Julian's murder.

"I thought you were getting a taxi home. How come you were walking?" Luke asked.

He groaned. "Barbie and Ken, the podcasters. They distracted me on my way out and I forgot what I was supposed to do. I thought it would be okay at this time of night. Until I saw who was behind me."

"Thank God you're all right. Don't take any chances like that again. Not ever."

Kat, the bartender, returned. "I've had a look at the CCTV. You can see him clearly coming into range, before making off. When the police arrive, I'll show them the footage."

Hudson thanked her.

"I hate that we have to take all these protections," she said. "But Blyham is a dangerous place."

"I wish I'd known that before I came here," Hudson said.

When the police turned up, they were a lot more attentive than the pair who had come to his apartment at the weekend. They listened to a everything he said, before looking at the security footage. It didn't restore his faith in them entirely, but it went some way.

"My car is outside," Luke told him when they were done. "Let me drive you home."

Hudson squeezed his hand. "Sorry, but that's the last place I feel like going. I was shut up in there going crazy all day yesterday. Can we go for something to eat, like we planned? Somewhere I can relax for an hour?"

Luke smiled reassuringly. "We can do anything you want."

After thanking Kat and the customers who had helped him, they left the bar. Luke suggested a family-run Italian restaurant that was one block over. "Otherwise, we need to head into the city centre, or back down to the waterfront."

"Italian sounds perfect. I'm ready to eat just about anything."

They had just crossed to the other side when Hudson's phone rang. If this was work-related, it would have to wait until the morning. He checked the display. It was DS Coppola. He answered straight away. "Yes."

"We've got him," the detective said.

Hudson came to a stop and gripped Luke's arm. "Wiseman?"

"Yep. We picked him up in town. Looks like he was heading for the railway station."

Hudson released the breath he'd been holding. "What will happen now?"

"Well, you can relax. For tonight at least. We looked into that old Stalking Prevention Order you took out and it still stands. It was made for an indefinite period. So, we can charge him with breaching that today and hold him in the cells for court tomorrow."

"And all the other stuff? Julian?"

"For now, we don't have enough evidence for that. We need to continue our investigation, but we'll be asking him about it and finding out exactly where he was last Tuesday. Let us do our job and, as I said, try to relax. He's going nowhere tonight."

"Feel better?" Luke asked when the call was over, and Hudson filled him in on what DS Coppola had told him.

"I suppose, yes. To some degree. It proves I didn't imagine seeing him on Saturday and he's likely behind all the mail I've been getting. But I doubt much will come of it. He'll probably get a fine when he goes to court, and told not to do it again."

"A night in the police cells might be just the shock he needs."

"We'll see." Hudson's optimistic tone failed to convince even himself.

They reached the restaurant, which was only around the corner and down the street from his apartment. Hudson realised how little of Blyham he was actually aware of. He was so caught up in his head, he was wandering around blind most of the time. He needed to open his eyes and appreciate where he was.

They were taken to a table in the window. It was Monday night, and the place was barely half full. A relief, as it meant the nearby tables were empty and they had a degree of privacy. A server brought the menus and asked for their drink orders.

"I need a proper drink," Hudson said. "If I order a bottle of wine, will you help me drink it?"

"I've got the car," Luke said. "But a small glass won't hurt."

They ordered a bottle of house red and a jug of water.

As he took the first sip of wine, Hudson finally relaxed. He murmured appreciatively at the flavour and sat back in the chair, stretching his spine.

"You're pretty amazing, you know," Luke said. "After everything that's happened in the last week, you still keep swinging. I imagine a lot of other actors would have been on a plane back to the US by now."

"I've never been a quitter." He took another sip. "But I'm not sure I'd be as upbeat as I am without you. Apart from Julian, you're the only person I've gotten to know here. I'd have gone crazy if I'd had to deal with this alone."

Luke put his elbows on the table. His dark eyes reflected the candlelight. "I'm glad you trust me. I'll always be here for you."

A surge of heat, excitement, rushed through him. A familiar feeling he associated with being with Luke.

The server returned for their orders. Hudson hadn't even looked at the menu. "I'll have a ham and mushroom pizza, please."

Luke ordered mushroom and truffle risotto. Then they were alone again.

A male couple outside studied the menu, debating whether to come in. One of them seemed keen, the other less so.

"What the hell is the Blyham Cat Killer?" Hudson asked.

Luke was about to try the wine, and paused, the glass halfway to his lips. He laughed. "Why do you want to know that?"

"Something Corman and Amber said earlier. That they interrupted their report into the Blyham Cat Killer to announce that *Darkest Blue* was coming to town. It sounded...weird."

"Hmm." Luke sipped the wine. "If you'd listened to their podcast you wouldn't say that. It's very random. They cover everything you can imagine. Local news, celebrity gossip, environmental issues, neighbourly disputes, school competitions, national headlines, health and beauty, fitness. It's like one of those nutty morning TV shows in podcast form. For some reason, a lot of people seem to like it. Mainly because of their charisma and personality on air. They are very good at what they do."

"And the cat killer?"

"Oh, that's exactly what it sounds like. Last year, there was a series of cat murders all over the city. The poor things were beheaded and left in places people would find them. Like park benches, footpaths, shop doorways, that kind of thing."

"Sick."

"Totally. I was really worried about Molly when it was going on. She's such a friendly little soul she would go up to anyone who approached her. Thankfully, she doesn't wander further than the few houses on our street. The cat killings were all within the city centre."

"Did they catch the bastard responsible?"

Luke shook his head. "But I don't think there's been any more since maybe last October. I guess whoever was responsible has either moved away or gone to prison for some other offence."

"Or progressed onto something bigger than little cats. That's how it works with these fuckers. They start with helpless animals before working their way up to hurting people."

Luke grimaced. "There are plenty of examples of that in this city."

"I need to start listening to *Beyond Blyham*. I feel very ill-informed."

The couple outside had eventually decided to come in.

"They've rubbed you up the wrong way, haven't they?"

"Huh?" Hudson asked.

"Corman and Amber."

"Oh." He pulled a face. "Just a little. They've got some kind of agenda going on. I don't know what it is, but it's not promoting the play, I know that much."

"Well, duh. The only thing they're really interested in promoting is themselves."

Hudson had already finished his first glass. He poured another. "I think you're right. I'm certain they're gearing up for a muck-raking job on my past."

"How come?"

"Ah, just a couple of things they asked me about earlier. Ancient history really. It's kind of odd they should mention it now." When Luke's brow furrowed in interest, he continued. "What the hell. I might as well get it off my chest. It starts with that fucking movie. *Red Hills Massacre*."

"Surely that's not so strange. They're bound to be interested with everything that's going on."

"That's just the start." He took a deep breath. This was not a story he'd ever shared before. Probably crazy to spill it to another journalist, but he trusted Luke implicitly now. "I was young when I made that movie. Just starting out. I hate the damn film now, but it was a really big deal for me at the time. The director was Singer Fry. He made it clear when they were casting that it was close between me and another actor. I'm not claiming to be a victim here. I wanted that role and did what I had to get it. Which included going to bed with Singer Fry."

Luke's eyes widened. "Hudson. I'm so sorry."

"Hey." He raised both hands. "This was well before Me Too. I knew that's what it took to get the job, and it was a price I was willing to pay. That was all on me. I'm not blaming anyone else."

"You weren't the one in the position of power. It was an abuse."

Hudson shrugged. "It was what it was. It's not the part I have a problem with. It was afterwards. Once we started shooting, Singer thought he could call on me whenever he wanted to have extra helpings. I don't know if you've ever seen the guy, but, well, all the Viagra in the world couldn't get me hard for him again. That's when the movie became a real nightmare. Long night shoots, take after take out in the cold woods in just my underwear, when I'd nailed the scene first time. Belittling me in front of the crew. Screaming, tantrums. The guy was coked off his tits most of the time, so he was volatile enough without the added sexual revenge."

Luke reached across the table. "I'm so sorry."

He shrugged. "Don't worry. That's not what this story is about. So, Singer was an asshole. Big deal. It was Hollywood. A major studio movie. I'd wanted the part. I gritted my teeth and got on with it. I finished the movie without sleeping with him again, it came out, was a huge hit, and I got a lot of offers on the back of it. It seemed a fair trade-off." Hudson swallowed a mouthful of wine. "My career seemed to take off afterward, each part better than the last. And at the same time, so did Singer's. Thankfully, our paths never crossed again, though I used to look at the hot young actors in his movies and wonder what they'd had to do to get their roles.

"I was around twenty-eight, twenty-nine when *The Leopard* came up. This was the biggie. A mega-budget superhero movie with franchise potential. I was shortlisted, then screen tested, then suddenly it was down to me and another actor, and after weeks of waiting, I got it. A career and life-changing moment, right?"

Luke looked concerned. "Well, I already know you weren't *The Leopard*. What went wrong?"

"The age-old Hollywood story. The director left the project after having problems with the studio executives. Two weeks before we were due to start shooting."

"Creative differences?"

"Exactly. And when he was replaced by Singer Fry, I was out too."

"Shit."

"I was disappointed. Of course I was. But it was what happened next that ruined my career. Stories began to appear in the press that the whole reason the movie had been delayed and the original director fired was because of me. That I was difficult and demanding. Stories backed up by people who claimed to have worked on the film. It was complete bullshit. I'd done everything that was ever asked of me for that role."

"Stories put out by Singer."

Hudson nodded. "It was around that time that I was outed too. I'm certain that came from Singer's camp as well. He wanted to ruin me completely. I'd heard rumours that he'd done the same to other actors who had rejected him, but now I got to experience it first-hand."

"Bastard."

"Powerful bastard. Still is. How many of those big fucking franchise movies has he made now? Each one bringing in massive profits. He's untouchable. As was I, in an entirely different way after those stories leaked. My days of playing romantic leads were through." He sighed. "In a way, it did me a favour. I moved into theatre and that's what I truly love. There's great money to be made in TV and film, but my heart is on the stage."

They were interrupted as their food arrived and the server made a big deal of grinding black pepper and adding Parmesan cheese to their dishes. It all looked and smelled fantastic.

"Good choice," Hudson said. "Coming here, I mean."

Steam rose from the plates, and they were both too hot to eat.

"So, what is it with Corman and Amber? You think they're planning to dig all of this back up again?"

Hudson filled his glass and offered a top-up to Luke. He put his fingers over the rim.

"I'm driving, remember?"

Hudson gave his best puppy dog look. "You could always leave the car where it is and stay with me tonight."

Luke hesitated a moment, before grinning. "Restraint has never been one of my virtues." He took his hand off the glass. "Go on then, fill it up."

Hudson splashed the wine into the glass. "I don't know what Corman and Amber are up to. But this morning's creepy mail delivery was a photo of me from *The Leopard*, then later today, they brought it up as well as asking about Singer."

"Could Robbie have sent you the photo?"

"Of course he could. The man is insane, I wouldn't put anything past him. But the only reason that I can see for the podcasters to be interested in Singer Fry is that they plan to put out some sensational scandal piece. They probably hope I'll give them an exclusive on sexual abuse and exploitation in Hollywood. Isn't that the kind of story that will bring their local podcast to international attention?"

"I hate to say it, but yes. That's exactly what they'd get from it."

"Either way, I don't trust them. This show is troubled enough, without having to worry about a couple of desperados digging into things from my past that I would rather forget."

Chapter Eighteen

Savage Streets

The meal was fantastic. Hudson and Luke followed the main course by sharing the house signature tiramisu dessert. By the time they'd finished, Hudson was still in no mood to return to the apartment.

"Let's grab a nightcap somewhere," he suggested after Luke insisted on paying the bill.

"Okay. The New Inn isn't far from here. I'm not sure what's on there tonight, but it's probably the best option."

"I'll defer to your expertise."

Hudson was feeling pleasantly buzzed after finishing the bottle of wine. As the meal had progressed and he'd adjusted to the idea of Robbie Wiseman spending the night in a police station cell, a sense of peace had descended on him. Why not make the most of it and enjoy the rest of the evening? By this time tomorrow, Robbie would likely be back on the streets, and he'd have his guard up again.

"I don't really feel dressed for going out," Luke admitted as they walked from the restaurant. "I've been wearing these clothes for work all day."

"That makes two of us," Hudson said. "We can have a shower when we get back to the apartment. Besides, you're hot, whatever you wear. I'm sure you'll still be the best-looking guy in this pub."

Luke laughed. "You already know you're onto a sure thing, right?"

"Can't I give you a compliment without having an ulterior meaning?"

"Oh, I'll take the compliment gladly. Don't worry about that."

The New Inn was just about dead when they arrived. There were seven other customers and a bored-looking older man behind the bar. Madonna's *Deeper and Deeper* played on the jukebox.

"Whoa. It's the land that time forgot," Hudson whispered.

"I warned you," Luke said. "It will be livelier along at Sash, or The Viaduct, but I can't say I'm in the mood for either of those tonight."

"Me neither. Let's have one drink here then we can head to bed."

They ordered two glasses of red wine and took a table.

Hudson grimaced when he sniffed the wine. It was a big come-down from what they'd had in the restaurant.

"This place gets pretty lively at the end of the week," Luke said. "Live DJs, cabaret, drag queens. Mondays are deathly just about everywhere."

"We should make a date to go back to The Blue Pearl," Hudson suggested. "I loved that place. The music, the atmosphere, the food."

"What about tomorrow night? We can go straight there from rehearsals. I'll work through lunch to make sure I don't have to go back to the office afterwards."

Hudson patted his thigh. "You have got yourself a date, Mr Kamal."

Luke leaned in and pecked him on the lips. "I'll have to get up early in the morning though. I need to go home for a change of clothes. I am not wearing these two days running."

"Maybe we should. If we both turn up wearing these tomorrow, it will look like we're doing the walk of shame. Give them something to gossip about."

"And Corman and Amber will have something else to put in their podcast."

"Ugh. Shit, I'd just about managed to forget about them. You're right. Fresh clothes it is."

The wine tasted almost as bad as it smelled.

A Girls Aloud song replaced Madonna on the jukebox. Another oldie, but not *that* old.

A man in his thirties sitting at the bar adjusted his chair while Hudson and Luke were taking. Facing them, he pretended to be reading messages on his phone, but from the angle and direction he was pointing, Hudson suspected he was filming. The asshole had obviously recognised him from the recent news coverage. No doubt his footage would be shared on social media in the next few minutes.

And possibly picked up by any reporters in the area.

"Ah, stuff this." Hudson put down the awful wine. "I can't drink that. How about we head back and take that shower? I've got something much better to drink for a nightcap."

Luke's eyes flicked to the guy at the bar, catching on to what he was doing. "Great idea. Let's go."

They turned their backs to the intrusive camera and left.

The night was still and warm outside. There was a dark blue cast to the not yet dark sky.

"Can you believe that dickhead?" Luke said. "It was clear as day what he was doing."

"I've seen worse. Experienced worse. Someone people just shove their phones straight at you. At least he was attempting to be discreet."

"Hmm. I once saw Sir Ian McKellen having a drink with friends during the interval of a show. People were just standing around him filming and taking photos, like he was some exhibit at a zoo. I can't believe how little they respected his privacy."

The streets were quiet as they walked deeper into the gay village.

A single car came past in the opposite direction. Hudson looked up just in time to see two faces at the passenger side windows staring directly at him. *Oh, shit. Surely that guy's video can't have alerted the press already.*

The car drove past them, followed by the screech of tires as it braked.

"Let's pick up the pace," he said to Luke. "I think we've been spotted."

Luke glanced backwards. "Yep. They're turning around."

They quickened their steps.

The car pulled alongside, kerb crawling. It had pulled onto the wrong side of the road to get closer to them. Hudson's danger senses prickled. He walked even faster.

The driver's window was down. "What's up, ladies?"

"Fuck," Luke muttered. "It's not the press. Ignore them and keep moving."

"Nice night for it, isn't it, girls?" the driver called.

"Cruising for cock, are you?"

Hudson couldn't stop himself from looking at them. The driver was a mean-looking bastard, all steroids and tattoos. In the seat behind sat a gingery blond with a full beard.

"Ooh, I think the old queen likes you," the driver called to the man behind.

Hudson simmered with anger and frustration. He knew the best thing to do was ignore them and get to the safety of the apartment. They just needed to reach the end of the block, turn the corner and they would almost be there.

"Hey," the guy in the back seat yelled. "Don't be so stuck up. We're only trying to be friendly. Why don't you stop and say hello?"

"Leave us alone," Hudson snapped, regretting the words as soon as they were out of his mouth. The last thing he should do was engage with these assholes.

"What's that?" the driver shouted. "American. We've found ourselves a real Yankie faggot tonight. Jackpot, guys."

"The other one doesn't look much like a Yank to me," a third voice from inside the car said. "More like an immigrant. Fresh off the small boats, I don't doubt."

"I think they both need to be taught a lesson and sent back where they came from."

"What the fuck is this?" Hudson hissed.

Luke grabbed his arm. "Just run."

They shot off together, racing for the corner.

As another car turned into the road, there was a screech of brakes as they tried to avoid the obstruction.

Two of the men were already out of the car and chasing after them. The blond guy from the rear seat and the side passenger, who was short and squat. The driver was engaged in a war of horns with the other vehicle.

Hudson and Luke raced into his road. The apartment building was in sight, still a distance away, and the men were gaining fast.

Of all the bad luck, there was no queue or security staff stationed outside of The Viaduct tonight. Their only option was to reach the front door of his building.

He glanced behind. The blond guy was fast on his feet. It was like being chased by a creature from one of his old horror films.

He couldn't believe this was happening.

"I'm going to tear your head off your shoulders and shove it up your arse," one of the men hollered.

Hudson was grateful for his own fitness. He wouldn't be able to hold his own in a fight with these pricks, but he could run without too much effort. Adrenaline and stress kept him powering forward. Thankfully Luke was at his side.

Hudson pulled his wallet from his pocket and extracted his key card before they reached the door. He swiped the electronic pad. The light stayed red. *Shit.* He tapped the card again.

He could hear the heavy pounding of feet behind then.

At last, the light turned green, and the lock released. Hudson and Luke tumbled into the lobby, shoving the door shut behind them. Putting all their weight against it, they waited for the lock to catch.

The two men thudded against the other side, pounding on the glass.

It was a relief to hear the soft click of the lock.

The taller man pounded on the glass with his fists. His face, twisted with fury, was even uglier than Hudson had realised. Spit spattered the window as he swore at them.

"Now we know where you live, motherfuckers," the smaller guy said, punching the door.

"And you're on fucking camera, assholes." Hudson pointed to the CCTV cameras that covered the lobby and the front door.

The small one was so stupid he gave a cartoon double take before tugging on his buddy's arm and dragging him away. The blond spat a huge green glob of spit at the window before eventually backing down.

"Fuck." Hudson leaned against the wall for support. His legs were suddenly weak. "What the hell was that?"

"That is the kind of behaviour that's gotten out of hand in this city these last few years. Right-wing bastards who think they can take their hatred to the streets."

"Are you okay?"

Luke's face was ashen. Hudson hadn't seen him look so drained.

He breathed deep and nodded. "Just...shocked. Fucking mad, too. How dare they? How fucking dare they behave like that?"

Hudson put his arm around him. Luke's entire body trembled. "It's okay," he said softly. "They're gone. It's safe now."

Upstairs, Hudson prepared them two stiff glasses of whisky, while Luke reported the incident to the police.

"For what good it will do," Luke said when he got off the phone.

"They'll get some clear shots of them from the cameras in the lobby. And there must be CCTV covering the main road. It's got to have picked up the car and its registration."

"That's all true. But it's also got to be worth someone's time and effort in the police to investigate and track them down."

"Surely things can't be as bad all that. Those guys came for us in public. It has to count for something."

Luke sighed, leaning into him. "I wish I shared your optimism. It's been like this for years now. It's getting worse, not better."

"You can report it? Put it in your paper."

"I will. I'm just not convinced it will lead to anything. And do you really want more of that kind of publicity?"

Hudson put a hand on his leg. "Well, straight answer — no. But that doesn't matter. Quote me all you want. I'll even give an interview. Maybe we can shame the cops into finding those pricks."

"You know who'll be all over it? Corman and Amber. They'll love championing the cause."

Hudson laughed and squeezed his thigh. "Maybe they'll be useful after all then." He sipped his drink. "Shit. When I signed on for this play, I had no idea that most of the drama would take place off stage."

"Let's hope that's the last of it."

"Now, that is optimistic."

Chapter Nineteen

The Empire Theatre

The following Monday, the production of *Darkest Blue* moved from the rehearsal rooms at the Blyham Concert Hall to the other side of the river and The Empire Theatre. Originally, they were due to have one full day to run the show on the main stage before it opened, but as the first night had been pushed back to Friday, they had the luxury of having four days to work on stage.

Hudson had been reading Luke's book about the history of the old theatre. Built in the 1920s, its original art deco style had been restored to the most glorious condition. In the last hundred years, the theatre had hosted some of the most highly regarded productions and actors in history—all of the Shakespeare greats as well as current hits of the day like *Cat On a Hot Tin Roof*, *Cabaret*, *Oklahoma!*, *West Side Story* and *My Night with Reg*. Luke's book was filled with stories of the great actors who had trodden the boards there, as well as the backstage troubles and scandals. The Empire had a colourful history, including rumours of at least five different ghosts that were said to haunt the old building, from the trap room beneath the stage, to the dressing rooms and auditorium. There was one in particular, believed to be the spirit of a former usher, murdered by her jealous lover after an affair with a leading man, who was frequently seen in the backstage corridors.

Hudson prickled with excitement when he walked into the theatre at nine o'clock that morning.

After the events of last Monday, the rest of the week had been relatively calm and had allowed him to focus on the play. Robbie Wiseman had been charged with breaching his stalking order. He'd been given one hundred hours of unpaid work and, in addition to the stalking order, he'd been excluded from entering Blyham city for the duration of the play's run. The investigation continued into whether he was responsible for sending the malicious mail to Hudson, but since his arrest, there had been no further packages. However, he was out of the frame for Julian's murder, having a firm alibi for that night.

The security cameras in Hudson's apartment had produced perfect, clear images of two of the men who had tried to attack him and Luke. Despite this, there had been no arrests or further update from the police since they had reported it. Luke had told him that the images hadn't even been made public on the Blyham police social media pages and websites. Despite the evidence, it seemed as though the case had been filed with no further action taken. Luke was pressing his editor to see if the paper could publish the photos and stories without the cops' permission.

Though he'd been shaken badly afterwards, Hudson had done his best to overcome the experience and get on with the job he had to do.

As he went through the stage door, Manuella and Sal arrived just behind him. Manuella had a huge smile on her face. The kind of smile that said she was getting great sex. Hudson had suspected his Spanish co-stars were getting close as Sal had settled into the production. It looked like they had sealed the deal over the weekend. He tried not to let the detail that she'd been getting close to Julian just before colour his opinion.

"Good morning," he said.

"Buenos días." Manuella beamed. She was glammed to the max with flawless, stage-ready make-up. She wore her dark hair up, and a strappy, printed summer dress which revealed lots of leg, arm and cleavage. There were lashings of gold chains around her delicate neck and multiple bangles piled up on both wrists. "This is so exciting. I can't wait to see the set."

"Me neither," he admitted. They had rehearsed with a rudimentary set so far. This would be the first time they saw the full construction and got to wear their proper costumes.

After his initial nerves last week, Sal had relaxed considerably. He had the same post-fuck glow as Manuella and looked handsome and confident in a light, open-necked shirt, linen shorts and leather loafers with no socks. The image of casual summer. "Hi," he said with a wide smile, fixing Hudson with his dazzling eyes. "I am word perfect on both of my roles now."

"That's good to hear." Hudson couldn't blame Manuella for wanting him — the man even set his own pulse quickening. "Shall we go see what this is all about?"

A theatre assistant led them through the backstage area. She was about to take them to their dressing rooms when Hudson asked if they could go straight to the stage. He'd waited long enough for this moment. Didn't want to put it off any longer.

It was always exciting, walking into a new theatre. Wherever he was in the world, the feeling was always the same. Soaking in the atmosphere. Even the musty smell of old wood was a pleasure. There was the excitement of what was to come, the potential for greatness in each new performance, merged with the history and prestige of what had taken place before.

"God, I love this," he said.

He heard familiar voices ahead. Andie was shouting, and Rav sounded like he was attempting to talk her down.

"Always arguing," Manuella remarked. "They should sleep together and get it over with. It will be better for everyone."

Hudson suppressed a laugh. Manuella hadn't picked up on Andie being a big old lesbian. Rav would be the last person she'd want to go to bed with.

They walked onto the stage from the left.

The first scene of the play took place in a hotel bar in 1974 in Barcelona. Hudson raised an instant smile at the set design and décor. The production team had nailed it, with sickening shades of brown, yellow and orange. If the furniture was not from that period, then they'd done a first-rate job at replicating it. The cushions scattered about the lounge area were an assault to the eyes.

"What are you shouting about?" he asked.

Andie and Rav stood by the bar. Her hair was wild, as though she'd been tearing her hands through it.

"This motherfucker," she shrieked, gesturing all around her.

178

"I think it looks great," Hudson said.

"It's too much," she cried.

"It's what you asked for. What you agreed," Rav said.

"I fucking hate it. It's an eyesore."

"You wanted genuine 1970s," Rav said calmly. "That is the setting."

"I know it's the fucking setting, but we're staging this *now*. I don't want the audience distracted by all this nostalgia crap. They need to focus on the play, not the set. It's not a fucking comedy. They'll think they've come to watch *Abigail's Party*."

Now that she had pointed it out, Hudson realised she had a point. Though first impressions were amazing, it was very kitsch. "Maybe just replace some of those cushions with something more timeless or modern. I'm sure it only needs a few tweaks."

Another voice entered the conversation. "Less would definitely give you a lot more. You should tear out all that period stuff and just use the basic bar set. Let the audience use their imagination of the rest."

Ugh. Amber.

She was sitting in the second row of the auditorium with Corman, who was filming the stage.

Andie dropped her bottom lip, breath hissing through her teeth. "Maybe she's right. We should clear all this crap out."

"No," Hudson said firmly. "The team have put a lot of work into this. Let's run with it today. We've got until Friday. We can make adjustments as we go. Swap things in and out if needed. Remember who the real creatives are. Here's a clue, it's not those damn podcasters."

From the side of his eye, he saw their faces glaring at him.

Screw the pair of you.

The first podcast about *Darkest Blue* had dropped on Friday. As Hudson suspected, the focus had been more on Julian's murder and the impact it had had on the cast and crew. Hudson didn't understand podcasts or how their ratings worked, but the release of the episode had resulted in a flurry of fresh interest. Reporters and photographers had appeared outside the apartment again, though not as many as before. Jo had pestered him with renewed calls for him to accept requests for interviews from TV and radio stations as well as all the national press.

It had been a relief to withdraw to Luke's place for the weekend and turn off his phone. No one had known he was there, and he'd been able to relax and enjoy quality time with Luke. It was the one bright spot in an otherwise difficult few days.

Hudson had resolved to stay well clear of Amber and Corman for the rest of the run.

* * * *

"There are two policemen here to see you."

Hudson groaned. After a busy morning, lunch was the first quiet moment he'd had. Luke wasn't due to join the rehearsal until this afternoon and Hudson had retreated to his dressing room for an hour of calm.

The room was pretty standard for an old theatre. Compact, with little natural light. The small window, high on the wall, didn't open, and on a hot July day, the place was stifling. He had two table fans running at full speed and had left the door propped open to get the air circulating.

"Send them in," he told the stage door attendant and hung up.

Lunch had been a tuna salad box, bought in from a nearby convenience store. He cleared away the empty wrappers and papers and finished his bottle of water when the detectives arrived.

It was DS Benito Coppola and Kris Peters, Luke's ex. *Terrific.*

The former was overdressed for the summer heat in a three-piece suit. Very smart, but totally impractical. Kris had removed his jacket and slung it over his arm. He'd unfastened his top button and loosened his tie. His white shirt clung to the swell of his beer belly. Both of them looked sweltering.

There were more bottles of chilled water in the mini-bar fridge beside his dressing table, but Hudson wanted to know why they were here before he offered any hospitality.

Apart from the dressing chair, there was a small leather sofa against the window wall. He gestured for them to sit.

Kris' sharp eyes stared at him attentively. Contempt was obvious in the downturned corners of his mouth.

"To what do I owe this unexpected pleasure?" he deadpanned. "Have you identified the guys who came after us?"

"Not yet," Benito said. He might as well have added *not ever*. His lack of interest could not have been clearer. "That's not why we're here. The investigation into the murder of your co-star is our priority."

Kris snorted. The line of his jaw was hard, full of tension.

Hudson ignored him and focused on Benito. "And have you made any progress with that?"

"We're getting there. We need to ask you some more questions." Benito was a very handsome man, but what kept him from being attractive was his officious attitude. Hudson suspected he was the kind of cop who considered everyone to be guilty until they were proven otherwise.

"About your relationship with Julian King," Kris added, delight at the question fused with derision for Hudson.

"I'm not sure what there is to tell you that I haven't gone through before."

"The two of you were close?" Benito asked.

"We were friends. Good friends, I would say, considering how short a time we'd known each other."

"You used to go out with him," Kris said. A statement, not a question.

Hudson prickled. "We went for food and drinks several times after work. Neither of us knew anybody here apart from members of the crew, so it made sense."

Another snort. "Didn't take you long to find someone, though."

Hudson spoke to Benito but pointed at Kris. "Is it appropriate that he's even here? Given his personal interest in me."

"The only interest I have in you, mate, is as a suspect," Kris said.

Benito ignored both of their remarks. "Did you ever go out for more than drinks and dinner after work?"

What the hell are they getting at? "No. Most nights I was back in the apartment by eight or nine at the latest. I don't know what Julian did after that."

"You knew he was bisexual?" Benito asked.

"No, as a matter of fact, I didn't. Though I don't see what difference it makes."

"According to his ex-wife, he was quite open about his bisexuality."

"So? He didn't talk to me about it. There was no reason he should."

"And it wasn't unusual for him to make friends when he was working away from home."

"Friends with benefits," Kris added with an immature smirk. "Were you one of those friends?"

Hudson took a deep breath. He'd love to wipe that look off Kris' face and couldn't believe the audacity of these incompetent fuckwits. When he spoke, his voice sounded amazingly measured and calm. "No. Julian and I were friends and nothing else. Whatever it is you're trying to imply, you couldn't be more wrong."

"I'm not implying anything," Benito said. "I'm asking. Were you having a sexual relationship with Julian King?"

"And again, for anyone dumb enough not to get it the first time, no, I wasn't." He stood. "And if that's all you've come to ask, you can leave so I can get back to work."

They took their time getting to their feet.

"And if this is as far as your investigation has gotten after two weeks, you should be ashamed of yourselves," Hudson added. "I've been looking into some of the things that have gone on around here in the last few years and it doesn't make for the nicest reading. Like the Blyham Strangler, among other things. You and your colleagues didn't come out of that smelling of roses, did you?"

Bentio stiffened. Kris' face was cold stone.

"I saw what happened then and I can see exactly what you're up to now. Using the victim's sexuality against them. Blaming them for their own deaths.

Because it's convenient. Because it's easy. What happens next? You probe around for a few more days before getting bored. Move on to another, juicer case. Move Julian's murder to the cold cases archive."

Bentio attempted to meet his gaze, failed and looked away. "Thank you for your time. We'll be in touch if there's anything else we need to ask you."

Bentio went straight out of the door. Kris lingered. His mouth was pinched. His fists clenched. After a moment, glaring at Hudson, he let out an ugly laugh and followed his partner from the room.

Hudson realised he'd been holding his breath and released a sigh of relief.

Another perfectly fine day had been ruined.

Sometimes, it felt like the whole of Blyham was trying to distract him from this play.

Chapter Twenty

In the Star Dressing Room

"Your ex-husband is an asshole."

Luke raised his brow in amusement. "That's one of the many reasons that he's my ex. You think I wasn't aware of the fact?"

"Sorry. It's just that the prick has really wound me up today."

It had gone four o'clock and rehearsals were on a break. Andie had followed Hudson's advice to leave the set as it was for most of the day, but before they were due to have a final run-through of the second act, she'd had a complete meltdown and insisted the entire thing be redressed. Hudson sat with Luke in the first row of the stalls, watching as the director and the set designer argued on stage over the changes.

Hudson told Luke about the visit he'd had from Benito and Kris at lunch time.

"Jesus," Luke said. "They really are the lowest. So what if Julian was bisexual? Does it make his death less important to them?"

"That's the impression I was left with, too. I have to keep reminding myself that they are gay themselves."

"They are career police officers first," Luke said. "Climbing the greasy pole comes before all else. They want easy answers, fast resolutions and another step closer to promotion. They won't see any kind of obligation to their community because they aren't part of it. The force is their brotherhood."

"It's depressing."

"I agree. Though I can tell you that not all officers are like that. The Blyham force is rotten to the core, no doubt about it, but there are some decent officers in there now, trying to make a difference. Unfortunately, they don't fit in with the old boys' crowd and aren't in any position to influence things."

"That's even more depressing." Hudson took hold of Luke's hand and placed it in his lap. "I'll tell you what's not a downer. You. I was so pleased to see you after lunch. I missed you this morning."

Luke gave a mock-shocked expression. "Wow. Coming from the man who wanted me barred from the project a couple of weeks ago."

Hudson leaned closer, grinning. "Yeah, well, a lot has changed in that time." He pressed his lips to Luke's.

"It certainly has." Luke returned the kiss.

Hudson murmured softly, enjoying the warmth of Luke's mouth, the tenderness of his touch. In a caring moment like this, all the stress and frustration of the day melted away, if only for a while. Hudson squeezed his hand. "Thank you," he said as they parted.

"For what?"

"For keeping me sane in this batshit city."

Luke trailed his fingers through Hudson's hair. "It's my pleasure. Though I don't think you've seen the city at its best."

"I doubt I could have experienced any worse."

Hudson regretted the words as soon as they were out, as they seemed to manifest Corman and Amber into being. The podcasters appeared at the end of the aisle, overkill smiles firmly in place.

"Hey, guys," Corman cheered.

"Aawh," Amber gushed. "You guys look so adorable together. I didn't realise you were a thing. I'm so happy for you."

Hudson bristled, but hid his irritation with a smile as insincere as theirs.

"We saw those two detectives earlier," Corman said. "Were they here about the murder?"

"Did they come to see you especially? Any news?" Amber asked.

Hudson ignored them. On stage, Andie was still locked in an argument with the designer, only Manuella had now involved herself in the decision-making. A lot of arms were being waved around and gesticulating. There was no way they'd be ready for the second act before five o'clock.

"Can you give us a scoop for the podcast?" Corman asked.

Hudson closed his eyes and breathed deep before speaking. "What part of stay out of my way didn't you guys understand? I have nothing to say to you, today, tomorrow or ever." He stood up and signalled to Luke. "Come on, let's go."

Hudson pushed past Amber and Corman, who were no longer smiling. He told Ruth that he would be in his dressing room once Andie was ready to start work again and headed backstage.

"Don't you think you were a bit abrupt with them?" Luke asked, catching up with him.

"I can't waste any more time on those people. I've made it as clear as the fucking sun in the sky that I don't want to talk to them, and they keep coming back. You heard that shit they put out last week. I'm not going to be any part of that."

"Fair enough," Luke said. "I'm pissed off at them for spoiling a beautiful moment."

Hudson laughed. "Yeah, if I'd started on them for that, they'd each be sporting a new asshole about now."

Luke took a frisky swipe at his butt. "I'm not really interested in their arseholes. Not when you're around."

As they entered the warren of backstage corridors, they almost walked straight into Steve, who, as usual, was glued to the screen of this phone.

"Watch it," he snapped, almost dropping the device.

"If you tried watching where you are going," Hudson said, "you might not get in the way."

Steve tutted, looking them up and down. "Where are you going anyway? I thought we were about to go through Act Two."

"Taking a break. Andie is still going at it with the set designers. We won't be getting back to work anytime soon."

Steve brandished his copy of the script in his other hand. "I need to speak to her about Sal. I don't think we need him in the martini scene. I can't understand half of what he says, so the audience will have no chance. I've got some ideas about how I can deliver the information instead."

Hudson jerked his thumb to the stage. "She's that way."

There was nothing wrong with Sal's delivery. Steve had been trying to build his own part from day one, despite being the only member of the cast to still blank on his readings. He wouldn't be happy until his role was big enough to claim star billing. In his own mind he already was.

They continued down the maze of gloomy passages. Hudson put his hands on Luke's waist and shoved him against the wall. This time the kiss was deep, open and passionate. He thrust his tongue into his mouth, grinding his body against him. Suddenly, sex and Luke were the only things that mattered.

Luke moaned and pushed his hips against Hudson's hardness. Luke was equally aroused. He gripped Hudson's head in both hands and rivalled his passion in the kiss.

Suddenly there was a noise from the direction in which they had come. Hudson froze, turning to see. The corridor bent sharply to the right. In shadows, he thought, just for a second, he detected movement. A face darting back around the corner.

"Hello," he shouted. "Anyone there?"

No reply.

"What's the matter?" Luke asked.

"Thought I heard something. Saw someone."

"Steve? There's no one there now."

Hudson called out again and no one answered.

"Strange. I'm sure I didn't imagine it."

"Maybe it was one of the theatre ghosts," Luke said lightly. He took Hudson's hand. "Come on. It's probably not a good idea to be snogging out here anyway. Not when you've got the star dressing room at your disposal. Lead me to it."

The room was as hot as it had been before. Regardless, Hudson shut the door behind them and turned on the two fans.

"I know a good way to cool off," Luke said, his fingers already unfastening Hudson's shirt. Hudson unbuckled his belt and tore open his trousers, shoving them down to reveal his gloriously hard dick. Luke grinned. "No messing about. I appreciate your enthusiasm."

Hudson lunged for another kiss, slipping his shirt from his shoulders, standing in front of Luke, just about naked. Luke's hands roamed across his back, pulling them together, escalating the tension.

"Andie could call me back to the stage at any minute," Hudson gasped between kisses. "No time to fool around. Not when I want you as badly as I do." His hands slipped beneath Luke's shirt. His skin was hot, damp with a light layer of sweat. He pressed his mouth to Luke's neck, tasing the saltiness. "Fuck me."

Luke hurriedly tore off his clothes, matching Hudson's passion, tossing them without care to the floor.

Hudson stumbled out of his shoes, shorts and underpants. His hard cock bounced against his belly as he hurried to the holdall he had stashed beneath the dressing table earlier. He pulled out a box of condoms and chucked one to Luke, who wasted no time tearing into the wrapper. Next, a bottle of lube. He pumped two good squirts into his hand, rubbed it around his fingers, before sweeping them through his ass crack. He rubbed the lube all around the opening, pushing inside before reapplying and going deeper. Luke had already fitted himself with the condom. Hudson applied lube all over his cock. Massaging the sticky fluid along Luke's raging length made him want it even more.

"Did you lock the door?" Luke asked.

He couldn't remember. "Who cares? No one will come in without knocking."

Hudson leapt onto the small sofa. He set his elbows against the backrest and pushed his ass towards Luke. Luke needed no other encouragement. He stepped up behind him and rubbed his cock up and down the length of his crack, sweeping over his hole, teasing him with its hardness. Hudson was excited. He shoved backwards, impaling himself on the head of Luke's cock.

Luke let out a deep throated moan. "You really are impatient."

"Get inside me."

Luke held his waist in both hands and slid in deep. Hudson groaned, surrendering to the sublime sensation, being so utterly penetrated. Sweat stung his eyes as he rocked back and forth, arching his back, giving all of himself to Luke. All the stress, all the complaints he'd had down on the stage were forgotten. They were meaningless. All that mattered was the beautiful man fucking him.

Their hot, slick bodies slapped and slipped together. It would be obvious to anyone coming close to the dressing room door what was happening inside. Hudson didn't care. He dug his hands into the back of the sofa and pushed back even harder, trying to take Luke deeper.

The frenzy could not be maintained. They were possessed by an urgency they could not control. The catch in Luke's cries, the erratic rasp of his breath, told Hudson that he was close to the end. "Come inside me," he demanded.

Luke cried, slamming his hips harder and harder against Hudson's ass. When Luke began to jerk and spasm, consumed by his orgasm, Hudson reached for his own cock. It hardly needed any stimulation. Just the sweep of his palm was enough to send him over. Cum spewed out of him in great, shuddering arcs.

"Oh my God," he cried as he convulsed through one ecstatic pulse after another.

Afterwards, when they had disposed of the used condom and cleaned up, Hudson was reluctant to get dressed. "Let's just lie here for a little while." He took Luke's hand and guided him back to the sofa. Sex had been the stress buster he'd needed — now he wanted to relax and savour the afterglow with the man who had come to mean the world to him.

They sat side by side, their bare feet propped on the small coffee table, allowing the two fans to ineffectually waft warm air over their hot skin.

"I bet this room is freezing in the winter too," Hudson commented.

"Probably. They spent a lot of money refurbishing the front-facing areas of the theatre, but if this is the star dressing room, it doesn't look like the modernization made it this far."

"I kind of like it, though. It has character. The rehearsal rooms were modern and comfortable, but they are too corporate. They've got no soul."

"I agree. I much prefer it here."

"Have you ever been in this room before?" Hudson wondered aloud.

"Well, surprising as it might sound, I don't make a habit of sleeping with the stars who perform here. So, this is a first in many ways."

They both laughed.

"Yeah, I don't make a habit of sleeping with hot journalists either."

"Given how highly you speak of the profession, that comes as no surprise."

Hudson raised Luke's hand to his mouth and kissed it. "It turns out, they're not all bad. In fact, I've met a really sweet one."

"That is good to hear."

And it was good to goof around. Luke made him laugh a lot and there had not been much reason for that of late.

Hudson hoped his good mood and good fortune would continue.

Chapter Twenty-One

"Not the Nice Guy That You Think He Is"

"No, no, no. Stop." Andie's voice roared from the darkness of the auditorium.

Hudson groaned inwardly. What the hell was wrong now? He disregarded her, and ignoring the hesitation on Manuella's and Steve's faces, he continued with the scene. His co-stars hesitated for a moment, looking uncertain, but got it back together and followed his lead. Steve was halfway through a complicated chunk of dialogue when Andie stumbled up the side steps onto the stage.

She clutched a heavily annotated copy of the script and a disposable coffee cup. Her hair was a mess. Her eyes were so puffy she seemed to stare out of swollen slits. He'd never seen her so wired.

"Didn't you hear me?" she bawled. "Stop what you're doing." She thudded to the middle of the stage, the boards trembling with each step.

"Andie," Hudson said, sounding calmer than he felt inside, "we don't have time for this. We need to get through it." The first preview was tomorrow and as yet, they had still not completed a single, uninterrupted rehearsal of the show. The current performance had almost made it to the end of Act One. Halfway through, Hudson had stopped waiting for the stoppage, daring to believe they would make it to the end unchallenged.

She shushed him with a wave of the script. "We can't open like this. People are paying good money to come and see this and what we've got is a messy piece of shit."

"There won't be anything for them to see if we're not given the chance to finish what we're doing."

"He's right," Steve said in a rare show of allegiance with Hudson. "All these interruptions are bullshit."

Andie turned her tight eyes on him. "You're in the theatre now, Mr Dillard, not one of your crappy, one-take TV shows. This is craft, and the only way to improve it is through being challenged."

Steve appeared on the verge of retaliation when Manuella calmed him with a firm hand on his forearm. Hudson realised they'd reached a desperate stage. Ordinarily he'd be the first one to call Andie out on her crazed behaviour and petty arguments, but they were so close to the first night, they could not afford it. He'd have plenty to say to her a few days after the opening, but this was not the time.

He'd been shocked by her complete unravelling in these last few days. Whether this was part of her normal directing process, he had no idea, but since they'd moved to working on the main stage, nothing made her happy. She'd pulled apart the character choices and directions she had given in the prior weeks. She hated the set, the lighting, and the sound. Rav had done an admirable job at keeping a lid on her worst behaviour, but even he seemed defeated today.

"I think you should be sitting on the other side of the bar," she said to Manuella, taking her hand and guiding her across the stage. "I want you here when Steve starts to speak."

Jesus, she stopped the show for that? Andie could have given Manuella a note for the next performance. Hudson knew better than to say it. It wouldn't take much to tip Andie into a full-blown argument and they couldn't waste the time. Steve appeared on the verge of saying what Hudson had been thinking. Hudson mouthed 'don't' at him and Steve was bright enough to take the hint.

After another five minutes of direction, Andie seemed satisfied and went back to her seat. They picked up the play from the start of the scene and made it all the way to the end of Act One without another interruption. Hudson breathed a long sigh of relief.

"Be ready for the second act in half an hour," Andie yelled as they left the stage.

"She's lost the fucking plot," Steve muttered as they shuffled into the wings.

"Just humour her to keep the peace," Hudson told him. "You know what you're doing and what you're doing is great. Just stick with what we worked on before and ignore this craziness. Everything will calm down after tomorrow."

"I hope you're right. I can't take much more of this shite. And certainly not four whole weeks of it."

Hudson went straight to his dressing room. He didn't want Andie to trap him and fill his head with more of her last-minute ideas. He needed time out.

Luke was not at the theatre that afternoon. He'd been sent a screener of an upcoming film release and needed time alone to watch it and prepare his review. They'd arranged to meet at The Blue Pearl at nine for a late dinner and a catch-up. No doubt Andie would insist they rehearse late, but as far as he was concerned, they shouldn't be making any changes to the show now. They needed to focus on perfecting what they already had. Working until midnight would only lead to more frayed nerves and tempers.

The dressing room was as hot as it had been all week. Hudson left the door propped open—without Luke's sexy ass, there was no reason to close it today. He put the kettle on and dropped a green tea bag into a mug. Despite the heat, he needed the tea to calm his frazzled nerves.

He flopped on the sofa while waiting for the water to boil. What a day it had been. He'd already experienced pre-opening jitters of his own, without Andie's full-on meltdown impacting every aspect of the show. *It's all good*, he told himself. Everyone on stage knew their characters and their lines inside out. Even Steve had got his act together. They knew what they were doing. And the backstage team were first rate. As long as they all did what they were expected to, nothing could go wrong.

It's all fine. Nothing to worry about.

He made the tea and added a good splash of cold water to cool it down.

Fifteen minutes of peace and quiet, then he'd be ready for the stage again, where hopefully Act Two would be flawless.

His ass had barely touched the sofa when a voice interrupted him.

"Hi, Hudson. Got a minute?"

From where he sat, he could not see the door, but Amber's simpering tones were unmistakable.

"No, I don't," he said, imitating her smarmy voice. "I'm busy and one more time—I don't want to talk to you. Nothing has changed on that front."

"It's really important," she said.

Before Hudson could reply, she walked into the room, followed by her living shadow, Corman. For once, they weren't smiling. Other than a tablet, neither of them seemed to be carrying any recording equipment.

"C'mon," Hudson said. "I'm trying to take a break here. You've seen what it's been like today. I need some time alone. Please, get out."

Amber clasped her hands in front of her, head bowed. He'd never seen this humble side of her. Something was off. Something he didn't trust. "It's really important that we speak to you. Now."

"While Luke isn't here," Corman added.

Hudson's senses sharpened. He studied the podcasters. What the hell were they up to now? What was so urgent that they had to speak to him in this private time between acts. And without Luke? He sat straight, muscles tensed and ready. "Come on then, what is it? And you'd better not be recording any of this."

They both shook their heads.

"We're not," Corman said. "Honest." He held the tablet up, screen forward, to show him there were no audio recording apps open.

Amber shuffled closer. Her eyes met his at last, filled with a strange intensity. "This is kind of awkward. We know you and Luke have got close."

"That's another fact that had better not make its way onto your podcast," he said.

"You've got the wrong idea, mate," Corman said. "We're here to help. Doing you a favour."

Hudson doubted they ever granted favours without requiring something in return.

"You only met him a couple of weeks ago, right?" Amber asked. "When you first got here."

He nodded, warily.

"And has he told you much about himself? About his past?"

For fuck's sake. What are these idiots playing at? "Look, it's obvious you've got something you want to tell me. Some dirt you've managed to dig up, hoping to provoke a reaction for your show. I'm not interested. If it's anything important, Luke will tell me himself, when he's ready. In the meantime, it's none of my business, and it's certainly not yours."

"The safety of this show and everyone in it is our business," Corman said. "Especially after what happened to Julian."

Hudson's suspicion of their motives deepened. "What happened to Julian?" His voice was laced with scepticism.

Amber and Corman exchanged a glance.

"He doesn't know," she said.

"We need to tell him."

Hudson's jaw tightened. He was losing his patience. "Oh, knock it off. Enough of the game playing. C'mon then. Tell me, whatever bullshit it is that you think you know."

Amber straightened up. "It's just that Luke…might not be the nice guy that you think he is."

"What's that supposed to even mean?"

"We think he's dangerous," Corman said.

"No," Amber said firmly. "We *know* it. He's very dangerous."

Hudson suddenly wasn't so sure. His anger dissolved, replaced by uncertainty. He felt bare beneath their intense scrutiny. "What is it you know?" he said at last.

"Has Luke ever mentioned a man called Reece Dempsie to you?" Amber asked.

"No." The name meant nothing.

"I'm not surprised." Corman tapped and swiped at the screen of his tablet, before handing it to Hudson.

It showed an old newspaper article. *Beloved father dead in ten-storey fall* read the headline. And below, the subheading, *One man arrested in connection with the death*. He scanned the date of the piece. Nine years ago.

"What is this?" he asked, unable to focus on the main text.

"Luke was the man they arrested," Amber said. "Reece was his boyfriend at the time."

"Reece fell from the balcony of his apartment. They'd been drinking and arguing. There were a lot of witnesses. They'd been to a party beforehand where things got out of hand between the two of them. Eventually they left, but the fighting continued when they arrived home. Neighbours above and below gave convincing evidence afterwards."

Hudson scrolled through the article. There was a photograph of a good-looking guy in his mid-twenties with a kid around five years old. He had short blond hair, blue eyes and an endearing smile. The child had the same features.

"That's Reece's daughter, Rose. She's sixteen now," Corman said. "We've spoken to her already. Poor kid wants answers that weren't provided at the time."

"He…what? Fell from the balcony?"

"That's not as easy as it ever looks in the movies," Corman said. "The rail was pretty high. You can't just fall over."

"And you think Luke pushed him?" he asked.

"The police did," Amber said. "So did the neighbours. And Reece's friend. And so does Rose."

"Luke was arrested. There was a lack of substantial evidence to prove it. Eventually, Reece's death was ruled by the coroner as misadventure. But that's not what anyone really thinks. Not then. Not now."

Hudson's hands trembled as he scrolled through the page. There was another photo of Reece. On his own. It looked like a holiday snap. He was smiling in the sunshine, in shorts and a T-shirt. Happy, carefree, thinking he had his whole life ahead of him.

"I don't see what significance this has on now." Hudson's voice sounded shaky.

"Don't you?" Amber asked.

"We do," Corman said. "Another man is dead in strange circumstances. And Luke Kamal just happens to be involved in a production of the play he was working on. It could be a coincidence. A mighty big one. But we don't think so."

"Luke didn't know Julian." The words were barely out of Hudson's mouth when he remembered the visit he'd had from DS Coppola and Luke's ex Kris. They'd asked if he knew Julian was bisexual. It had seemed odd at the time, like they were desperately trying to make a case.

But what if there was more to it than that?

What if Luke and Julian had known each other? Or even deeper than that. What if they'd been lovers?

The small dressing room seemed to close in around him, while the floor felt like it had disappeared.

Had he been sleeping with Julian's killer all along?

Chapter Twenty-Two

More Secrets

Somehow Hudson got through the second act of *Darkest Blue*. The lines were ingrained in his mind, and he completed the rehearsal on autopilot. Though Andie halted the show several times to criticise one thing or another, she appeared to be oblivious to his lacklustre delivery. When she eventually called it a day, he hastened from the stage without waiting for her notes. His head and heart were already somewhere else.

Hudson hurriedly changed out of his costume into a light shirt and trousers and rushed from the theatre. He'd texted Luke earlier to say he'd be done sooner than planned and needed to see him before nine o'clock.

He was still in a state of shock over the facts Corman and Amber had presented him with. Rationally, he managed to reason that Luke had no reason to tell him about the death of an ex-boyfriend. It was the best part of ten years ago. Who would want to dredge that up with a guy he'd only known for a few weeks? On the other hand, Luke had been arrested for murder, and given the current situation, the podcasters had planted sufficient suspicion that Hudson couldn't shake it off.

The waterfront was busy when he reached it. The exterior tables of the bars and restaurants were all packed. The early evening sunlight cast a shimmering hue over the river and the buildings all along the bank were bathed in a golden glow. Hudson's troubled mood couldn't have been more at odds with the joyous beauty of the setting.

Luke leaned against the rail on the riverside with his face turned towards the sun. The sight of him in profile took Hudson's breath away. He'd never looked more handsome, like a hero from a romance movie. He turned as Hudson approached, his beautiful face breaking into a radiant smile.

"Hey," he said, stepping forward with open arms, coming in naturally for a kiss.

Hudson sidestepped the attempt and put a hand on his biceps. The smile he gave in return was stiff and awkward.

Luke sensed the change immediately. "What's wrong? Don't tell me something else has gone wrong. How did the run-through go?"

Hudson glanced around. Thankfully, no one was paying them any attention. Now that he was here, he didn't know how to handle this. He turned away from Luke, put his hands on the railing and glared into the water. It was easier if he didn't look at him. He inhaled.

"Tell me about Reece Dempsie," he said at last.

Luke's intake of breath was audible. "It was a long time ago. How do you...? Oh, of course. Amber and Corman."

"You're not denying it, then?"

"Denying what? What have they told you?"

"That he was murdered? That you were there."

"Fuck me," he said, exasperated. "That pair are unbelievable."

"Then you're telling me it isn't true?"

Luke moved up beside him, leaning on the railing. "Reece wasn't murdered. *I* didn't kill him, if that's what you're getting at. Don't tell me you believe those arseholes?"

"I don't know what I believe anymore." Still unable to look at him, Hudson stared at the rippling patterns on the water. "How about you tell me your version."

"My version," Luke retorted. "Jesus. You want me to go over all of that again. Do you know how painful it is?"

Part of Hudson wanted to back down and comfort him, but his guard was already up. He needed to protect himself. Luke had been his sole comfort in the last few weeks. The one he'd turned to, who had helped him handle all the troubles — Julian's death, the return of Robbie Wiseman, the difficulties with the play, being in a strange city. He'd overcome his initial reservations to trust him, to love him even. What if that had been a mistake?

"I need to know," he said flatly, feeling like a bastard, unable to change course.

Ten, fifteen seconds passed before Luke spoke. "Reece fell from the balcony of his apartment. I assume you know that, and that part is all true. But I didn't push him over. The police questioned me about it. More than once. It's the version of events they preferred, but they could never prove it because that's not what happened." He sighed and took another moment to gather himself. "Reece's bloodstream was filled with alcohol and a concoction of different drugs — cocaine, temazepam, Ecstasy, cannabis, I can't even remember them all now. I bet Amber didn't mention that part."

Hudson shook his head, still staring at the water.

"That figures. The police weren't keen to release the info to the press at the time either. It wasn't made public until the inquest. Reece had a long history of drug and alcohol abuse. He managed it well most of the time. Even I wasn't aware of it when we first started dating."

"How long were you together?"

"Not long. About eight months. I met him when I was living in Leeds. Reece had a lot of issues — sex, drugs, alcohol — but despite it all, he was still a charming man to be around. In the beginning at least. He was honest with me from the start. Told me he'd gotten married to a local girl when he was nineteen to please his family. He didn't want them to know he was gay. He never did tell them. When everything came out afterwards, they refused to believe it. They blamed me for corrupting him, among many other things. Reece had been having sex with guys in secret since he was seventeen. He was twenty-six when we met. Divorced by then, but he had a good relationship with his ex and his kid. They were probably the most stable influences in his life. He managed to keep a lid on his demons when he was around them."

Finally, Hudson looked at Luke. Luke did not return his gaze. Now his eyes were fixed on the water. When he spoke again, his voice wavered.

"I often wondered if he would have been happier staying with them and living a lie. He would probably still be alive now, I'm sure of that. He wanted to have sex with men, so many men, but it never seemed to make him happy."

"Is that why you were arguing? On the night he died."

Luke stiffened, obviously wounded by the question. Something twisted inside Hudson too. He knew that he was hurting Luke right now, but he couldn't stop himself. It was a callous act of self-preservation.

"No," Luke said flatly. "We were arguing because I'd decided to end it. After eight months, I couldn't cope with his erratic behaviour. When he was sober, he was a dream, but the sober moments became fewer and fewer. Whatever was the root cause of his troubles, it was clear that I was never going to be the one to help him resolve them. He was too closed off from me."

The moment was interrupted by a shrill scream behind them. Hudson spun in shock.

Two women were arguing in the one of the nearby bars. They were on their feet, screeching insults at each other, while four of their friends attempted to intervene. A drink was thrown, leading to greater roars of protest. Ignoring them, Hudson turned back to Luke.

"Go on."

"Things reached a head at the party. I decided it was over for good that night, but I didn't want to announce it in front of all those people. I figured I'd do it afterwards, but then Reece got drunk and started belittling some of the serving staff. A thick streak of casual racism also ran through him, another charming point I only learned later in the relationship. Funny, really, that I didn't see it earlier. When I first told him my family was from Morocco, he made a remark that he thought I just had a great suntan. Anyway, I pulled him up for the way he'd spoken to the staff and the argument kicked off from there. I intended to leave, but my friend, whose party it was, pleaded with me to take him with me. He'd gotten so shitfaced he wasn't welcome anymore." Luke sniffed. "So, I agreed to take him home. I got him back to his apartment and made a pot of coffee, which he refused to drink. He opened a bottle of vodka instead. The argument from the party reignited and that's when I told him we were done. That's what the neighbours heard us shouting about. He threw the cup at the wall. It was the usual nasty break-up you'd expect when alcohol is involved. I wasn't aware at the time that he'd also taken coke and the other drugs at the party."

He paused. The story was difficult to tell. Hudson wanted to believe him. Needed to believe him. He studied Luke's face, searching for signs that he was lying. His sincerity seemed obvious, but to Hudson, an actor used to faking a convincing emotion, uncertainty remained.

"And then what happened?"

"I left." Luke's voice had developed a cold edge. "I put my key on the coffee table and let myself out. By the time I reached the ground floor, Reece was dead on the pavement outside. I was the one who found him. Who called for an ambulance. But it was already too late."

"I'm sorry." The words sounded meaningless.

"For months I blamed myself for what had happened. Not in the same way everyone else blamed me. I knew that I hadn't pushed him over that balcony, but I was consumed by guilt. That what I had said provoked him. That I should have spent the night regardless of what we'd fought over. That I had a responsibility to look after him. I'd seen him in far worse states than that, and yet I knew I'd failed in a duty of care to him."

"Why didn't you tell me before?" Hudson's voice betrayed his doubt.

"Why should I? It's not something I go around broadcasting. I spent years afterwards being consumed by guilt. By what ifs. It's something private. Something hurtful. I would have told you when I was ready. And in the middle of an investigation into Julian's murder, that time wasn't now."

At that moment, two women approached them. "Excuse me, Hudson," the older woman said shyly. "Would you mind taking a selfie with my daughter?"

They regarded him with nervous but hopeful smiles.

"Sure," he said, going through the motions of being a celebrity. He posed for a couple of photos, waited while they checked they were happy with them, wished them well.

"We're coming to see the play in two weeks' time," the daughter said, grinning from ear to ear. "We can't wait."

They had provided a welcome distraction.

"You're looking at me like you don't believe a word I've just told you," Luke said when they had left.

"I'm just… I don't know. It's floored me, that's all."

Luke reached for him. "Hudson, why should it change anything? For Christ's sake, we're grown men. There's a lot of things in both of our pasts that we don't know or talk about."

There are no dead boyfriends in my history book. "Did you know Julian before he was killed?"

"What? Of course I did. I've told you before, I've seen him on stage and in loads of TV shows."

"That's not what I mean." Something inside Hudson told him to stop, to keep what he was about to say buried deep, but the words came out regardless. "Did you know him personally?"

Luke took a step backwards, his mouth hung open, as though speechless, then he said, "No. Why are you asking?"

Hudson's mouth seemed to take over from his brain. "The night I first met you, in The Blue Pearl, I was there with Julian. You didn't know him?"

"What the hell are you suggesting here?"

He gasped and turned back to the river. "I don't know. It's just a feeling I can't shake now."

"You're suggesting I killed him, aren't you? Oh, my fucking lord, you are. What possible motive could I have for killing Julian? Unless you think I'm a fucking serial killer who just goes around bumping off other men. Is that it? Do you know how insane that sounds?"

"I don't know what's what anymore," Hudson yelled.

"You should know I'm not a murderer." Luke flung his arms wide. "How could you even think that?"

"I've just told you," he said quietly. "I don't know what to think."

"I'm sure I do. Those idiot podcasters have found out what happened to Reece. They've put two and two together to make a fucking hundred. Exploited a tragedy—two tragedies, if you include Julian—and you've bought their bullshit theory hook, line and sinker. For fuck's sake, Hudson, I credited you with some intelligence."

Hudson put his hand on his forehead. The pressure felt like he was about to explode. "I need time to think."

"I'd say you do, too, because you haven't given this crap much thought at all." Luke took several steps away before turning back to him. "I thought we had something special. More than special. More than just a casual affair."

That's what made this so damned painful. They did have something special. Hudson had fallen in love with him.

But had that love made him blind?

He closed his eyes and tried to shut out all the noise.

"I can't do this," he said at last. His voice was tremulous. Hot tears pricked at his eyelashes.

"Hudson, take a breath."

"Luke, I'm sorry. I'm sorry for doubting you, but it's all become too much. The show starts tomorrow and I'm in no condition to focus on anything but that. Not with all this going through my head." Tears rolled freely down his cheeks. "This... We need to stop."

"What? No, please."

He wiped his eyes. Shook his head. "I can't do this." His chest was unbelievably tight. It felt like he was being crushed. "It's just... I'm sorry, Luke. But it's over. I can't go on."

Before Luke could stop him, before he could change his mind and take the words back, Hudson turned and hurried away. He didn't look back.

Chapter Twenty-Three

Luke

Luke wanted to run after him. To beg, plead and convince Hudson that he'd gotten everything wrong. That Amber and Corman had only given him a fragment of the story.

But he stayed glued to the spot, heavy with the weight of what had just occurred. What had been said.

Hudson was right. Not about Luke or what had occurred nine years ago in that high-rise apartment in Leeds, but about the show. Hudson had to stay focused on *Darkest Blue* and make it his priority. To overcome this stress and be ready for the first preview tomorrow. The official opening night was just days away, when the nation's theatre critics would be in attendance, looking for excuses to eviscerate the production. Luke hoped he would be there too, to give Hudson — and the entire cast and crew — the acclaim they deserved, but for now, the best thing he could do was allow him some space.

Himself too.

He also needed time to think.

Luke felt a chilling shiver run through him, despite the warmth of the summer evening. His emotions were threatening to engulf him. Everything had been going so well with Hudson, but suddenly a chasm had opened between them. How had it come to this?

Surely Hudson didn't seriously believe he'd had anything to do with Julian's death. Hudson was overwrought, consumed by strain and the moronic doubts Amber and Corman had put into this head. What a pair of fucking idiots. Were they so wrapped up in their podcast ratings that they were prepared to derail the play just to put out an episode that would get people talking?

Depressingly, the answer to that was yes.

Luke turned away from the river. He wouldn't go after Hudson now. Maybe in the morning he would chance a phone call, but tonight they were both too angry to talk this through any more than they had. He'd learned through painful experience that nothing was resolved in anger.

He walked past the two women who had asked Hudson for a photograph. Noticed the way they were looking at him. He ignored them. Ignored everyone, forging a direct route to where he had left his car. Hudson was struggling under the pressure of so many people wanting a piece of him. He needed a break. Luke didn't blame the selfie hunters. People like that were the ones who bought tickets and decided the ultimate fate of any show, whether it ran or folded early.

He groaned as he walked. The pain in his chest was real. It seemed to fill his ribcage. Made his breathing difficult. His heart hurt.

Luke had known that he was falling in love with Hudson all along. Neither of them had ever said as much. It was only now, after their first genuine argument, that he realised how profound his emotions had become. And turning away from him created a hurt he had not foreseen.

Luke adored Hudson. He'd been a fan of his long before the chance of sitting in on *Darkest Blue* had ever arisen. He'd always found him handsome on screen, but when he'd first seen him in a live stage show several years earlier, he's realised how incredibly sexy he was. The cameras did not do justice to his smouldering good looks. But it was more than physical appearance. Hudson had a charm, an intense charisma that was intoxicating and could only be appreciated in person.

Luke had been crushed when Hudson had rejected him that night in The Blue Pearl. He'd built up the meeting so much in his mind beforehand. He'd spied him across the bar having drinks with Julian King and had deliberated for a long time whether to approach them. Luke was no celebrity hound. When he recognised an actor outside of work, he valued their privacy and left them in peace. But he'd been so captivated by Hudson and overcome with excitement. It hadn't seemed like anything bad to introduce himself before he left.

Hudson's rebuff had been like a punch in the guts.

He'd had no clue that he hated journalists so much. Plenty of famous people did, but the vitriol of Hudson's attack seemed so personal.

And then in the days afterwards, when Luke had managed to thaw the ice between them, and started to melt his heart, Julian had been killed.

And now Hudson suspected he might have been responsible.

"Fucking hell," he muttered. The idea of that was insane.

Luke hadn't lied to him. He didn't know Julian in any personal way. They certainly hadn't ever been lovers. The notion was ridiculous. Even if he had known Julian was bisexual, he still would not have been interested in him.

Luke crossed the road and made towards the alley where he had left the car. He passed by The Blue Pearl where he should have been having dinner with Hudson tonight. There would be other opportunities, he assured himself. His relationship with Hudson had gotten off to a difficult start and they'd overcome it. Luke was determined to win him over again.

The bar was busy. Lively music came through the open doors and windows.

This wasn't the time to dwell on what he was missing out on.

He was forced to step aside as two couples came along the pavement towards him with no intention of giving way. The man and woman in front showed a faint smile of gratitude as they passed. They second couple didn't even look at him.

But the man caught Luke's attention.

He was tall with gingery blond hair and a beard. Muscular and attractive. Only there was something familiar about him. Disturbingly familiar.

Luke turned to watch him walk away.

Last week, when he and Hudson had been attacked by the three men in the car, the man on the passenger side had had a very similar appearance. It had all happened so fast, but Luke had gotten a better look at him later, when they'd watched the CCTV footage captured in the foyer.

Is this him?

The man had an arm draped possessively over the shoulder of his girlfriend. He wore a pale yellow T-shirt, revealing tattooed forearms. Just like their attacker.

Luke was torn. Did he go after him? *And do what?* He wasn't even sure this was the same man. Get a photograph of him? Compare it to the security cam footage?

By the time he'd considered all his options, it was already too late.

The two couples had disappeared into one of the bars further along the waterfront.

Damn. He'd missed his chance. Had it been him? Or just a random stranger with a similar appearance?

He ran his hand through his hair. Perturbed, he continued on his way to the car. He couldn't have challenged the bloke on his own anyway.

In all likelihood he'd been mistaken. His nerves were on edge after what had happened with Hudson, and he was imagining things.

Much like Hudson had today.

Christ. He'd accused him of killing his ex and maybe murdering Julian too.

His car was parked in the shade of an alleyway behind The Blue Pearl. Music blasted as he started the engine, and he shut it off immediately.

Now that he was alone, in private, tears were threatening to come. His breath was choked. The prospect of losing Hudson was more overwhelming than he'd ever expected. Especially on the basis of such a dumb misunderstanding. It was ludicrous, and proved that Hudson didn't know him at all. Luke detested violence. He'd spent his entire life avoiding it. The murders throughout the city in recent years, the escalation in abuse against the LGBTQ+ community—

it was all sickening. He hadn't known any of the victims of the Blyham Strangler personally, other than a slight acquaintance with the manager of one of the city bars, but their deaths had all hit hard. He'd mourned each of them. Then a string of separate killings earlier this year when young gay men had been the primary victims, it was all too much.

He sighed and rubbed his eyes. Hudson couldn't really believe he was a killer. He was stressed out of his mind, that's all. Luke would make him understand once the weight of the next few days had passed.

He turned the air conditioning up to max and started on his journey home.

This morning, it was a journey he'd intended to be making with Hudson.

Now they both faced the reality of an anxious night alone.

Reece's death had devasted Luke. Their relationship had been short and fraught with problems. He hadn't understood the full extent of Reece's drug and alcohol misuse. Like many addicts, Reece had been an expert at hiding it from those close to him. In the beginning, it had been fun. Reece had been a lively, boisterous drunk. Full of fun and humour. He'd encouraged Luke to drink to excess and stay out and he'd enjoyed it for a while, still young enough to handle the late nights and make it to work the next day.

Good times like that couldn't be sustained for long. It was when Luke objected or wanted to cut back that the problems began.

In the eight months they were together, Reece never gave any indication as to why he got so drunk, other than that he liked a good time. Anyone who challenged him or tried to curb his excesses was labelled a killjoy.

Luke couldn't keep up with his lifestyle and it was inevitable that they would break apart.

They had fought at the party on the night of Reece's death. The only reason Luke had insisted on accompanying him home was to save face for both of them. Reece's behaviour had gotten out of hand, and he'd embarrassed everyone with his crude language and unwanted attention. Luke had naively thought he could get him home, calm him down, then break up with him the next day when he was sober.

Reece had sneered and needled him the whole time and when they'd reached his apartment, Luke hadn't been able to stand it any longer. He'd snapped. Told Reece it was over right then. He was so used to seeing him drunk, he'd thought nothing of his welfare when he'd stormed out of the flat. He'd just had to get away from him.

It was the biggest mistake he'd ever made. The greatest regret of his life.

He'd heard the screams from the balconies above when he'd reached the ground floor and found Reece's body outside.

Nothing he'd experienced before or since compared to the horror of that moment.

Hudson had not been wrong on one count. Luke had been arrested and questioned by the police following Reece's death. The timing was too suspicious for them not to. Thankfully Reece's building was well covered by security cameras inside and out. The time codes showed that Luke was on the stairs, down to the first floor, when Reece fell from the balcony.

He was no longer under suspicion, but it did nothing to relieve his guilt.

If he'd stayed that night, they would surely have argued more. It would have been ugly, petty, but Reece would still have been alive afterwards, and Luke would have broken up with him in the morning. That one outburst, the momentary lapse of control when he'd blurted out that they were finished and stormed out of the apartment, had altered everything.

Luke had been repenting that ever since.

After he'd married Kris, and it had become apparent that his husband had alcohol and anger problems of his own, Luke had been determined not to repeat the mistake. It was an opportunity for him to do something right. To help Kris in the way he hadn't been able to for Reece.

He'd stayed in a difficult, toxic marriage for far longer than was good for either of them, out of fear for what would happen if he left.

Ultimately it had done neither of them any good.

As he turned onto the coastal road, Luke realised he'd driven most of the way on autopilot. He'd been so absorbed in the past, he'd paid little attention to the route. He smacked himself about the face. *Get it together.*

Another accident would solve nothing.

He would get home, take a shower, then try to put his head in order.

He couldn't react on stupid instinct like he had before. It would take careful thought and words to get his genuine version of events across to Hudson.

Maybe they both needed a couple of days to cool down before he even tried.

The sun was dipping low on the horizon when he pulled onto his drive, casting beautiful lights across the sky and water. It would have been a perfect setting for romance under different circumstances.

With a weary sigh, he got out of the car and locked it.

The street was deserted. Maybe Molly would visit him later. The cat had an uncanny knack of appearing whenever he was down and needed cheering up. He'd leave the front window open so she could let herself in.

He stood for a moment, looking out to sea, breathing deeply and reminding himself how lucky he was.

This evening had been a blip. A misunderstanding, contrived by Corman and Amber to generate controversy. A new sensation for their show.

He refused to give them that pleasure.

He would make things right with Hudson by the weekend, and they would d be left with nothing to report.

Luke had his keys in his hand when he approached the front door. As he inserted one into the lock, an unexpected noise alerted him. It came from the right side of the house.

Molly?

"Hello?" he called. No reply. An inexplicable unease skittered down his spine.

He turned the key when the sound came again.

Then a figure appeared from around the corner.

A figure wearing a baby-faced mask and carrying a lethal-looking knife. Silently, the figure tilted its head, as if studying him.

For a second, Luke was frozen. It was *the* Baby Face, the killer from *Red Hills Massacre*.

This can't be real. But it was.

He fumbled with the key, struggling to open the door.

That's when the figure with the knife raced towards him.

Chapter Twenty-Four

"Come Now"

After talking to Luke, Hudson was even more conflicted than ever. His life felt like it was falling apart. First Julian, then the return of Robbie Wiseman, now Luke. The first public performance was less than twenty-four hours away and he didn't know how he was going to get through the rest of tonight, let alone tomorrow. He called the only person he had left to turn to. Rav.

Rav suggested Hudson meet him the in bar of his hotel, but Hudson insisted they needed privacy for what he had to say and, after some reluctance, Rav gave the number of his suite and told him to come straight up. Hudson wrung his hands and gritted his teeth as he waited for the elevator to rise. People got on at every floor, going up. It seemed strange until he realised the hotel had a terrace bar and a restaurant on the top floor.

Another night and that would have been perfect. But not this one.

By the time he reached Rav's suite, the ball of tension in his guts had only constricted. He rapped on the door. Rav's smile was tight-lipped when he opened.

"What's the big emergency?" he asked as Hudson strode past him into the room.

"I don't think I can go on with this." Getting the words out was a struggle. His breath was shallow and fast.

The lounge area was bigger than the whole of the apartment Hudson was renting, with a large seating area, bar and dining table. Sliding doors were open onto a balcony. Hudson could see all the way across the river. The roof of the Concert Hall was visible from here.

"What do you mean?" Rav asked, following him through. "The previews start tomorrow. We open on Monday."

"I can't do it." He paced the floor, doing laps around the expansive coffee table. He punched his fist into his open palm. "It's all gotten too much."

"Hey." Rav came towards him with open arms. Hudson changed track to avoid him. "What's got into you?"

"I told you days ago this whole production is a mess, but you wouldn't listen. We had enough to cope with, with Julian's murder, and a replacement actor, but you just kept piling it on. Reporters, podcasters — you kept adding shit on top of shit. Expecting us to work through that. To learn a fucking show and deliver a performance."

"Hudson, what is this? You're not yourself tonight."

"Don't pretend you know me. You've ignored everything I've said from the start."

"Have a seat. Come on, let's talk this through."

"I don't want a seat," he snapped. In that moment, he heard his own voice. He sounded crazed. A diva actor having a meltdown. He paused in front of the open doors and fought to get his breathing under control.

"Have…have you spoken to Andie about this?"

"I don't know where she is. She's not answering her phone."

"Let me try her."

"No," Hudson said firmly. "I want to talk to you now. If you bring her in, the pair of you will gang up on me and nothing will change."

"Okay." Rav put his phone on the coffee table. "A drink, then?"

He closed his eyes and took several deep breaths, tuning out the chaos for a few moments. At last he said, "A whisky, just a small amount of water."

"Sure," Rav said, rushing to the bar, seemingly more confident now that he had something to do. He put two crystal tumblers on the granite counter and pulled a bottle from underneath.

After several deep breaths, Hudson turned from the window and joined him. He picked up his drink, swirled the glass, took a tasting sip, then downed the whole thing. He gave Rav the empty glass for a refill.

"Shit," he said. "This time tomorrow, I'll be on the stage. We'll be coming to the end of Act Two."

"And you'll be great. You always are."

"Don't bullshit me now. You were there this afternoon. You saw how bad I was in that last run-through."

"You were fine. There were a lot of other things going on. I've worked with Andie many times. She's always like this in the days before an opening. You'll see. By Monday night, everything will be a dream."

"As opposed to the nightmare it's been so far."

Rav pushed him the second drink. He put his elbows on the counter, looking at him earnestly across the bar. "What's got into you today? Have you received more of those strange letters?"

He shook his head. He was almost certain Robbie Wiseman had been behind the packages. The letters had stopped straight after Robbie's arrest. There had been so many other problems, he'd almost forgotten about him. "You need to get rid of Amber and Corman. If I see them at the theatre tomorrow, you'll have to prep Sal for the first performance because I won't go on."

"We need the —"

"Publicity. Is that what you think? Because we don't. And certainly not the kind of publicity they intend to bring. They are out to publicise themselves and nothing else. They're looking for scandal and dirt anywhere they can find it. And if I buckle under the pressure of this show, who's going to be right in the heart of it to capitalize on the disaster?"

"I'll have a word with them tomorrow. I'll tell them to stay out of your way."

"No. You will tell them to piss off and not come back. I mean it, Rav. There are too many distractions right now. The cops are still investigating the murder of one of your cast, in case you'd forgotten."

Rav's confident demeanour looked bruised. He sighed and ran a hand over his thinning hair. "All right. I'll take care of it. You don't have to worry about them anymore. I'll make sure that you, that everyone, gets the space they need to pull this show together. It's too important to lose focus now."

Hudson smiled gratefully. It had taken several weeks, but at last Rav was getting it. It would also mean Luke was out of the room too. For the next few days, that could only be a good thing. Hudson didn't know how he felt about Luke now, and what might happen between them. They needed space as well. Maybe by this time next week, he'd be ready to start again, if Luke was willing to. Fuck, he'd all but accused him of killing Julian. Hudson hadn't believed that for a moment. He'd allowed Amber and Corman to wind him up and had reacted in the exact way they'd wanted him to.

He wouldn't blame Luke if he didn't want to see him again. Not after that. But he couldn't dwell on it now. He had less than twenty-four hours to get his head together and deliver the performance that a full house of people had paid to see.

"I have never been this close to burnout before a show has even opened," he admitted. He took a sip of the second drink.

"You might not realise, but producing this car crash has not been easy either."

They both laughed, finally releasing the tension.

"And to think we want to do it all over again in London," Hudson said.

"We'll get there. We've had a run of bad luck, but once we open and the great reviews come in, we'll be rolling."

Hudson wished he shared Rav's confidence. Reviews were something he didn't have the bandwidth to deal with. Getting through those first shows without another disaster befalling them was the priority.

His phone vibrated in his pocket with a message notification. He ignored it. "If you clear the theatre of all but essential people tomorrow, I think we can get one solid rehearsal under our belt before the punters come in."

"It'll happen. Don't worry about it. Finish your drink, go to bed, get a good night's sleep, and let me take care of tomorrow."

Rav's phone vibrated on the coffee table. It was never-ending. Almost ten o'clock and people were still trying to get in touch with them. Unlike Hudson, he didn't ignore it, crossing the room to scoop up the phone.

Hudson took another sip of whisky and savoured the vanilla-tinged flavour. Rav was right. When he'd finished the drink, he'd book an Uber to take him home.

"What?" Rav said, staring at his phone screen.

Hudson groaned inwardly. *What now?*

"It's from Luke," Rav said. "I don't understand."

Hudson groaned. "It might be my fault," he admitted. "We had an argument earlier tonight. I could have handled it better. It wasn't my finest moment."

"*Need to see you about the play. Come now, or it won't go on. Urgent,*" Rav read. He squinted, as though not sure of what he was seeing.

"Huh?" Hudson pulled his phone from his hip pocket. The message he'd received was also from Luke. He tapped it open. "It's identical."

"What's it supposed to mean?"

"I have no idea." Hudson hit the call icon. It rang several times before Luke's voicemail kicked in. "It's me," he said. "I got your message. What's it about?"

He ended the call and glanced at Rav, whose brow was furrowed.

"Now what?" Rav's voice was tinged with concern. "What does it mean? The show won't go on."

Hudson shrugged. The knot of worry in his stomach had returned, even tighter than before. "I have no idea. By come now, I assume he means the theatre?"

Rav shook his head. "It's all shut up. There's no show tonight. They locked the doors when I left."

"His house, then?"

"It sounds serious. We should probably go."

What was Luke playing at sending such a cryptic message? And why wasn't he answering his phone afterwards? "All right, let's go. I'll get us a cab."

"My car is downstairs. It will be quicker." Rav grabbed his keys from a bowl on the counter and headed for the door.

The elevator ride to the basement garage was quicker than the journey up. Once they were in the car and out on the road, Hudson tried Luke's number again. It went to voicemail once more. "Shit."

"Do you know the address?" Rav asked.

"No, but I've been to the house a few times now. I think I can get us there. Head onto the north road out of the city then follow the signs for the coast."

Rav's hands were tight on the wheel. At the last minute he realised he was in the wrong lane, cutting across and earning an angry blare from the horn of the vehicle behind. Hudson's heart beat faster. The impression that something was seriously wrong grew stronger. He called Luke again and got no response.

"What the fuck is he thinking of?" Rav asked angrily. "As if we haven't got enough to worry about already."

Once they were closer to the coast, Hudson's directions became sketchy. He'd only ever come out this way as a passenger in Luke's car, and as such he'd paid little attention to the road numbers, roundabouts, or turnings. They ended up in a small village he did not recognise and had to backtrack a mile before getting onto the correct route.

"I recognise this now," he said, glad there was still a decent amount of light in the dusky sky. In complete darkness, he would have had no clue. "Keep going this way."

After another three miles, the sea was on their right, and he recognised the small street of houses overlooking the beach.

"This is it."

Rav slowed down until Hudson pinpointed the exact house and swung the car onto the drive. Luke's car was already parked up and there were lights on in the front window.

"I guess he's home," Rav said, shutting off the engine. "This had better be worth the journey here."

Hudson stepped out. He expected Luke to come rushing to meet them, but there was stillness from the house. The air was fresh with the salt of the sea, but there was an uneasy heaviness in the atmosphere that he could not account for. It gnawed at Hudson's nerves.

Rav joined him and they stared at the house. It was familiar to Hudson, and yet something was off. Then he realised the front door was open.

"Where is he?" Rav asked, his voice lower.

Hudson's stomach churned. The instinct to get back in the car and flee was strong. Something was very wrong here. His mind flashed on Julian's murder, and he was seized with a sudden panic. Something had happened to Luke.

"We need to find him."

He was already making for the door when a sudden movement to the right brought him to a stop.

He recognised the Baby Face mask in an instant.

Then a flash of steel glinted in the low light. An axe.

He screamed, "Rav, watch out."

Rav had no time to react. With three powerful strides, the movie killer was upon him. The axe swung from a high angle and made a sickening impact with his head. Blood splattered wide.

However violent the movie had been, the reality of the attack was far worse than it had ever been in the film version.

Chapter Twenty-Five

Evil Intent

Rav didn't scream. He let out a stunned grunt as the axe impacted. He wavered for a few seconds. Hudson took a step towards him, desperate to help, when Rav dropped to his knees then fell face forward, the axe buried in his skull.

It was over. Like a light being switched off. One second Rav was there. The next he was gone.

Hudson stared into the blank visage of the Baby Face mask. A monstrous character that had plagued his career and his dreams for two decades. And now his reality.

The killer gripped the handle of the axe, put a booted foot on Rav's shoulder and yanked it free with a sickening crunch.

Two dark eyes glistened from behind the mask.

Hudson ran.

He'd once played a character who fell victim to this monster. Not this time.

He shot through the open front door and slammed it behind him. The bulk of his pursuer thudded against the other side. Hudson reached for the key in the lock, but it wasn't there. Keeping all his weight against the door, he searched for an alternative. There was a deadbolt. He twisted the knob, and the bolt shot into place.

The door held when he stepped away while the killer rattled the handle.

He drew a quick breath of air. His heart hammered and it seemed like there was no space in his lungs. Outside, the handle continued to rattle. Then the killer kicked the door. The whole frame jarred but held. It wouldn't take him long to find another way in.

Hudson had a slim advantage.

He had to find Luke, if he was still alive. The alternative wasn't an option. He scouted around for a weapon but found nothing in the hallway.

"Luke," he yelled.

He was answered by a muffled sound. Upstairs.

He mounted the stairs two at time, yelling Luke's name again, following the reply.

Please be all right. If that bastard had done anything to him, Hudson would kill him himself, or die trying.

The lights were off on the top floor. With the encroaching darkness outside, the landing was long and dim, filled with shadows and dark open doorways.

He found him in the bedroom.

It was another image from a horror film.

Luke lay on the floor. He was tied to the arms and legs of a chair and must have tipped it over in an attempt to get loose. He was naked except for a pair of tight white underpants. *Just like in the movie. Just like Julian.* Something had been stuffed in his mouth and fastened around in a makeshift gag. He stared at Hudson with wide, terrified eyes.

At least he was alive.

Hudson managed to pull the gag free from his mouth and down over his chin.

"Are you all right?" he whispered.

"I think so." His voice was dry and raspy.

"He's outside. He killed Rav." He examined the bonds around Luke's wrists. Plastic cable ties. No way he could pull them apart. "Do you have anything up here to cut these?"

"Bathroom cabinet," Luke said, then coughed. "Nail scissors."

Hudson raced to the bathroom, thankful that he'd been here before and knew his way around. The small room was dimly lit but he didn't want to turn on the light and alert the killer to their whereabouts. He tore open the cabinet door, his hands shaking as he fumbled through the contents. Bottles and packets fell out. There was a clatter of steel on the floor. He dropped to his knees and finally found the small scissors.

They were tiny. Useless as a weapon, but they should be enough to cut Luke free.

He returned to Luke's side.

It sounded like the killer was using his axe on the front door. It wouldn't take him long to get inside. They had to work fast. If they could get out the back while he was still preoccupied, they might stand a chance of losing themselves in the fields beyond. Enough time to hide and call the cops.

He started working on the cable ties, the small scissors barely making an indent on the tough plastic.

"Do you know who it is?" he asked. "Did you see his face?"

"No. He was wearing the mask when he jumped me. It's fucking Baby Face."

The first tie snapped. Luke raised his hands, gripping his fingers while Hudson started on the second wrist.

"Is it Robbie Wiseman?" Luke asked.

"I didn't get a good enough look. It happened so fast. He killed Rav without a second's remorse." The second cable fell away, and Hudson got straight to work on his ankles.

As soon as Luke was free, Hudson helped him to his feet. His legs wobbled and he leaned against him. Hudson tried to check him over in the fading light. It looked like he might have taken a beating, but there were no obvious wounds.

Hudson helped him into a pair of jeans and a T-shirt.

"We have to go, now."

His heart seemed to stop as they made their way down the stairs.

Baby Face had vanished. Mercifully the door had withstood the onslaught of the axe. Would the rear entrance hold up so well? The windows?

They crept down to the hall, listening all the time for the sound of breaking glass.

Luke was steadier on his feet when they moved stealthily into the living room. Hudson turned off the light so they couldn't be seen from outside. He passed his phone to Luke. "Call the cops. Tell them to get here fast."

Hudson moved to the window, peering around the curtains. It was near dark outside. Ominously quiet. Every shadow contained the threat of death.

"Police," Luke gasped into the phone. "We need help, right now. There's been a murder. Someone is still after us."

Hudson could hear the calm voice of the emergency responder on the line. Luke gave the details and his address. How long would it take them to reach here? Five minutes? Ten? Hudson's breath was deafening in his own head, and he strained to listen further, for anything outside, or something in the house that should not be there.

Suddenly the outside security light came on and the whole driveway was illuminated. The two vehicles and Rav's body, lying face down in a widening pool of blood.

Hudson shrieked as a face appeared at the window. Baby Face.

Only a pane of glass separated him from that blank plastic mask. It was a perfect replica of the one worn by the killer in the movie. Even the costume — the blue overalls — was a match, but, in the harsh light of the driveway, Hudson saw the dark, wet stains of blood.

Baby Face lifted the axe and tapped it against the window. The blade scratched the glass and smeared it with blood.

"Shit. Hudson, get back from there."

He could only stare with a morbid fascination. Like a fox caught in headlights on a back country road, he was frozen to the spot. He gazed at the eyes inside the mask, hoping to see some recognition. Grasping for something.

Then Baby Face took a step back and swung the axe.

Amazingly, the toughened glass held, and the blade sprang back. Baby Face swung again with even greater force. It wouldn't stand up to much more.

"We need to get out." Hudson grabbed Luke and ushered him into the kitchen. There was still a chance they could escape out the back way and make it over the wall.

Hudson's shoes squeaked on the tiled floor. There were plates and mugs on the draining board, seeming so mundane, so utterly normal in contrast to the madness behind them.

"Keys," he gasped, noticing that they were not already in the lock.

Luke pulled a bowl across the table towards him, rummaging through the clutter.

The breaking sound of glass filled the house. The front window had given in.

While Luke scrambled for the keys, Hudson tore open a drawer, searching for knives. He found tea towels and dishcloths. *Shit.* The next drawer down was filled with jars of herbs and spices, rolls of cling film and foil.

"I've got it," Luke exclaimed, the key in his hand.

They lurched for the door. Luke took hold of the handle and was about to insert the key, when a figure appeared on the other side. Even through the frosted pane of glass, the Baby Face mask and overalls were unmistakable. They stepped back together.

Then, alerted by a sound from behind, Hudson spun to see someone else in a Baby Face mask enter the kitchen from the other end.

His heart seemed to freeze as his mind raced with so many colliding thoughts.

There were two of them.

Robbie Wiseman was not working alone. He'd found an accomplice. A mind as damaged and warped as his own, to share his love of that terrible film.

Hudson turned again at a noise from the door. The back door swung open, revealing the second Baby Face.

Instead of an axe, this one carried a lethal-looking butcher's knife. They raised their left hand, revealing the key they'd used to get inside. They let it jangle, taunting them, before dropping it. It rattled on the hard tiles.

"Robbie," Hudson said, glancing between the two figures. One of them was bigger, more well-built. That had to be Robbie, the first Baby Face with the axe. Rav's killer. "Take off the fucking masks," he said angrily. "We're not going to be part of this dip-shit reconstruction."

The second killer tapped their knife against the counter, then drew the blade along the granite surface, creating a high-pitched noise that set every nerve on edge. The bastard was toying with them. Teasing. Getting a kick out of the fear they generated.

Hudson backed against the counter, feeling for the drawer behind him. Was this one of the ones he'd searched already?

The first attacker jerked the axe towards him, threatening but not ready to hurt him. Not yet.

"Why don't you say something?" Anger governed the fear in his voice. "Come on, you've waited all this time. You must have something you want to tell me."

A gentle tilt of the head. It was a gesture lifted straight from the movie.

Had Robbie lost himself completely? Did he believe he was Baby Face now?

Hudson pulled open the drawer behind him and reached inside. His hand closed around a wooden spoon. *Fuck.* He searched again, feeling blindly, and found a plastic spatula.

They were screwed.

"Luke," he whispered. "I'm so sorry."

If they hadn't met and started a relationship, Luke wouldn't be in this danger now.

The two masked killers came closer, their weapons raised. The axe swung straight at Hudson. He dropped to the floor, feeling a whoosh of air as it missed his head, smacking into the counter.

He rolled away but the second killer was fast. Suddenly they were on top of him.

The knife was raised, coming down on him with deadly precision. In that second, he saw the evil intent behind the mask.

Flat on his back, unable to move. The blade came straight for his heart.

Chapter Twenty-Six

A Matter of Survival

The second killer's breath rasped behind the plastic mask, and it sounded so much worse than it ever had in the movie.

Hudson grabbed their wrist as the knife came closer to his chest. Baby Face clamped on with both hands, with the benefit of having their weight above him. The knife inched closer and closer. In a film, this was the moment the director would call cut, and Hudson would be replaced by a special effects prop. Not this time. That deadly blade was destined for his flesh.

He gasped and twisted, trying to wriggle free.

Those eyes bore into him, emitting pure evil.

There was a sudden, dull sound and the force above him relaxed. He glanced beyond the Baby Face mask. It was Luke. Hudson realised he had a wine bottle. Luke swung again and the bottle struck the back of his attacker's head. Hudson took advantage, yanking their wrist to the side, diverting the angle of the knife.

Undeterred, the first killer raised the axe, but Luke was too fast for them. He swung the wine bottle like a cricket bat against their head. There was another dull sound as it smacked against the mask and the figure staggered backwards. Amazingly, the bottle didn't break.

Above Hudson, the second attacker had regained their strength. A lithe body struggled against Hudson's, forcing a knee into his groin as they wrangled for control of the knife. He yelled in pain but refused to relax his grip. This was no superhuman killer from the film. It was a very real person—crazed and hellbent, but vulnerable just the same.

Luke smacked them on the head with the bottle again. Still, it did not break, but there was a cracking sound, whether it was bone or glass he didn't know. The killer might have been dazed but they did not weaken for a second. Another knee into Hudson's groin and pain boomed all through his body. For a few moments, his head swam, his vison blurred. If he lost consciousness, he would be dead. He was aware of the blurred flash of a blade, scything through the air towards him.

Then a sudden, hot wet eruption over his face and neck.

He heard a dreadful, choking sound. As the pain in his groin eased and his sight became clearer, the horrific realisation of what was happening sank in.

The broken neck of the wine bottle protruded from the throat of his attacker—blood spurted from the wound in rapid shots.

Hudson screamed and struggled out from under them. The tiles were slippery with blood and wine.

Luke reached for him, pulling him away, and the figure in the Baby Face mask rolled onto their back. Their body jerked in a series of uncontrollable spasms, coating the kitchen cabinets with a fresh paint of blood. Trembling hands grasped hopelessly at the broken bottle.

Hudson scrambled to his feet, gripping the counter, searching for the other assailant, the one who'd had the axe. They had vanished.

"Are you all right?" Luke asked, gripping his shoulders. "Did they get you?"

Hudson realised he was covered in blood. "No." He ran his hand across his wet chest. There were no injuries. "The blood isn't mine."

They looked at the figure on the floor. The horrific shuddering of the body had ceased. All that remained was a still heap, the blue overalls soaked in blood, a red pool widening on the floor around them.

"Where did the other one go?" he asked.

"Back through the front."

"Still in the house?"

"I don't know," Luke said. "They just ran that way."

Hudson looked at the knife, still held by the person on the floor. They needed to arm themselves but there was no way he wanted to touch that. He tore open one drawer after another, at last finding Luke's stash of kitchen knives. He pulled out the biggest two. When he turned around, Luke was crouching over the still figure.

"What are you doing?" Hudson gasped.

"I want to know who it is."

"We should wait for the police?"

"Fuck that. There's no sign of them yet. I want to know who the hell is behind this."

Hudson knew it was wrong to touch the body — Luke might already be held responsible for their death, and the less he had to do with the corpse the better it would be for him, but Hudson was also possessed with a deep hatred and a desire for the truth.

Luke gripped the bottom of the mask. Hudson didn't stop him. He drew it upwards over the face.

Recognition was instant.

Amber's head lolled to one side. Her mouth was slack, blood drooling down her chin. Her eyes were lifeless pools.

"Can't say I'm surprised," Luke muttered.

Hudson shook his head. Amber, a cold-blooded killer. It made no sense. "Why?"

Luke stood up, his eyes hardening as he took one of the knives out of Hudson's hand. "That's what we need to find out."

"No. We need to get away from here. Wait for the police."

"They'll come to the front." Luke gestured to the open back door. "Let's get out that way and go around the side. First sign of Corman—let the bastard have it. Don't hesitate. We'll worry about the consequences later. It's a matter of survival first."

Hudson couldn't tear his gaze away from Amber as he stepped over her body. His mind was reeling, trying to make sense of the discovery.

"The bastards must have stolen my keys one day during rehearsals," Luke said. "Had them copied and put them back in my bag before I noticed they were gone. They've had the damn thing planned for weeks."

There was enough light from the kitchen window and open door to see the rear garden and the path that ran down the side of the house. Hudson scoured the deep shadows beyond, looking into the cover afforded by the well-established shrubs and trees. They hesitated, listening. There was nothing but the breeze stirring the branches, and the more distant sound of the sea.

Luke tugged his sleeve, pulling him towards the path.

They progressed slowly, listening all the time for Corman, if it was him behind the other Baby Face mask. *Jesus, what kind of sick mind identifies with that kind of fucked-up character?* The kind who had murdered Julian to recreate one of the film's key scenes. Only that hadn't been enough. No, they'd had to go further. Just like the movie, they'd needed to increase the body count to get their kicks.

Evil bastards.

They reached the front of the house.

Where were the cops? How long did it take to respond to a murder call?

The security lights were still on, illuminating the entire front drive.

Rav's body lay undisturbed in the broad pool of blood.

"They killed him?" Luke whispered.

"He didn't have a chance. They jumped him as soon as we arrived."

Hudson looked all around for signs of the killer. Just like his movie idol, this Baby Face was a master of concealment, until the moment came to strike. When he'd attacked Rav, he'd come from the undergrowth along the side of the property. Was he hiding there now?

"Is that Rav's car?" Luke asked.

"Yes."

"Keys?"

With dismay, Hudson pointed to the body. "He had them on him when we got out."

Luke spun his head in either direction, tightening the grip on the knife. "Okay." He bit his lip. "If we get his keys, we can lock ourselves in the car until the cops arrive."

"Or get the fuck away from here."

"Even better," Luke said.

They approached slowly. Hudson stayed alert, trying to look everywhere at once. The front door of the house was open. *Shit.* It had been closed earlier. He checked the broken living room window. There was nothing but darkness within. Corman could be hiding in there too. He could come at them from anywhere.

Every shadow seemed to contain danger. Every rustle of the leaves made him edgy. Cold sweat trickled down his spine. He glanced at Luke, who appeared just as tense, but showed a steely determination to survive.

As they moved forward, they stepped into the pool of blood that surrounded Rav's body. Luke was not deterred. His courage strengthened Hudson's resolve too. They were going to get through this. Get out of here and make sure Corman paid for everything he and Amber had done.

Luke stood confidently, feet apart, the knife held steadily in front of him. "Get the keys," he said. "I'll cover you."

Hudson didn't hesitate. He squatted over Rav's body and tried not to look at the brutal mess that was his head. Rav was lying face down, his arms splayed beside him. Hudson couldn't remember what he'd done with the keys when they got out of the car. Had he kept hold of them? Put them in his pocket? He checked his hands first. The right was open, palm facing upwards, empty. The left hand was clenched into a fist.

"I'm so sorry," he whispered, taking hold of his hand. Rav's skin was still warm. "I'll get the bastard who did this to you. I'll make them pay."

Carefully, he unfurled Rav's stiff, bloodied fingers. There was no car key.

"They must be in his pocket," he told Luke.

"Keep looking. I've got you."

Fighting against his natural squeamishness, Hudson put his hands beneath Rav's hips, squirming to feel his pelvis and thighs, searching for the sharpness of a key. There was something hard in the left pocket. He pulled his hand back, feeling for the opening of the pocket, sliding inside. What he pulled out was a phone. From the right side, he produced Rav's wallet. He put them both to the side and slid his hands back into the pockets.

"I can't find the key," he said in frustration, still searching, going deeper.

Suddenly, he was caught in the glare of headlights, dazzled by the full beam.

He turned his head, screwing up his eyes as the engine roared.

He knew instantly that Corman had the key and was behind the wheel of Rav's car.

The noise was deafening. The glare of light became even harsher as it came towards him, the dazzle painful.

His hands were stuck beneath Rav, trapped in his pockets.

The car bore down on him.

He heard Luke scream, then his hands were on his waist, pulling him upwards.

For a second, Rav's full weight came with him. Hudson struggled, wriggling, finally pulling free. By the time he got to his feet, it was too late. He braced for impact.

He had no sense of himself in the next few moments. A sudden force. Then flying through space, rolling. A rush of something passing beneath him.

As he struck the ground and his whole body jarred with pain, his ears were filled with the grinding of metal.

As he lay on the ground, unable to move, he knew what had happened. Corman had crashed into the back of Luke's stationary car. He opened his eyes, blinking to find some focus. It was all a blur.

His vision slowly returned. And with it, a sinister silhouette against the haze of the wreckage. *Corman.* Each step forward was staggered, but he held the axe with menacing confidence. Hudson tried to move, but pain rooted him to the ground. He couldn't even raise a hand.

Corman's face came into focus. The Baby Face mask hung on a string around his neck. His face was bloody, one eye closed, but his expression was filled with cold determination. In that moment, it seemed like Corman no longer existed. He'd been taken over by the Baby Face persona and was living out his twisted dream. About to make a long-held fantasy come true.

He straddled Hudson's waist, licked his swollen lips, and raised the axe.

Hudson prepared for the inevitable.

As Corman's axe began its last, deadly descent, a figure loomed behind him. Luke, battered but determined, raised something in both hands. He swung hard. Hudson heard the impact and a smashing of ceramic as it exploded on Corman's head.

The force of the blow swept Corman sideways, knocking him off his feet.

The axe clattered to the ground, missing Hudson by inches.

Corman was on his knees, rising to come at him again. Then Luke was there, smashing into him with fast-moving fists. Luke roared with rage and anger as his jabbed the killer again and again.

Hudson's focus began to waver. The lights, the sounds began to blur.

In the distance, what sounded like a police siren.

Could be a TV, he thought fuzzily.

And then the dizziness overwhelmed him before he fell down into darkness.

Chapter Twenty-Seven

Getting Answers

Despite the impact of the collision, Hudson was fortunate that his injuries were no more serious than a fractured coccyx and severe concussion. He was kept in hospital overnight for observation.

"Where's Luke?" he asked the nurse who attended him the following morning.

"I don't know who you mean," she said with a concerned smile. "The police want to speak to you, but the doctor has forbidden it until he gives you the all-clear. He'll be making his rounds soon."

Hudson shuffled up the bed, wincing at the pain in his lower back, and eased his weight onto his side. His head was woozy. He didn't know if that was from the knock he had taken, or the drugs they had given him. Either way, he felt like shit. Despite all that, he had a clear memory of everything leading up to the crash last night. Rav's murder, Amber, Corman, those vile masks.

"I want Luke," he said. "I'm not speaking to anyone until I know that he's okay."

The nurse frowned. "Try not to get yourself agitated and I'll see what I can do."

When she left, he gripped the rail on the side of the bed and pulled himself fully over onto his left side. That felt better. He'd known a stuntman once who had broken his coccyx several times over. Hudson had thought he was exaggerating about the pain—now he realised he had underplayed it.

At least he was alive.

Thanks to Luke. If he hadn't attacked Corman when he did, Hudson wouldn't be here. He'd have ended his days with a split skull, dying on that driveway beside Rav.

Poor Rav. His family must know the devastating news by now. Their whole world would have collapsed.

His mind flashed back on those moments. Corman in the Baby Face mask, appearing as if from nowhere, bringing the axe down without a second's remorse or hesitation. The startled look on Rav's face, a few seconds of incomprehension and then nothing. That image, that memory would haunt Hudson forever.

And now what? Had Corman survived? Where was Luke? The police would want him for sure. Luke had killed Amber. Without Hudson's account, they had no evidence that it had been in self-defence.

He had to speak to them now.

He pushed onto his elbows, reaching for the buzzer at the side of the bed. "Nurse," he yelled. "Nurse."

When she came in a few moments later, she was not alone.

Luke came in behind. He looked exhausted, with sunken eyes and sallow skin, and was still the most beautiful thing he'd ever seen.

"Thank God," Hudson cried.

Luke ran to him. They wrapped their arms around each other. He could tell that Luke was holding back, fearful of hurting him, so Hudson hugged him even tighter.

"Are you all right?" Hudson said, choking back tears.

"I am now." Luke pressed his face into the crook of Hudson's neck. Hudson felt his tears on his skin.

"Are you hurt? The car..."

"Barely glanced me," Luke said, drawing back to look at him. He brushed his fingertips gently across Hudson's lips. "Oh, my God. Your face."

Hudson let out a relieved laugh. "I dread to think. But it doesn't hurt as bad as my ass."

Now they both laughed. Luke put his hand on his shoulder. "Thank God you're alive. When I saw you go over the roof of the car, I thought that was it."

"Corman—how did you...?"

"Smashed the bastard over the head with one of my plant pots. I hit him so hard, it shattered the damn thing. I only wish I'd hit him harder."

"Where is he?"

"Not here. They've taken him to a hospital in Newcastle."

"Alive, then?"

"Very much. Bleed on the brain, they say, but he's expected to pull through. He's under police guard. He won't be going anywhere other than prison when they discharge him."

Hudson gripped his hand and pressed it to his face. "What about you?"

He shrugged. "On police bail while they make enquiries. Fair enough, I suppose. I know how the system works. I've been at the police station all night, answering their questions."

"No way. That's not fair. They would have killed us."

"Hey," he said softly. "Don't get so worked up. The cops know what happened. They're just doing their job. Making sure they have all the facts. I've never been the biggest fan of Blyham police before, but they've been fair with me. I'm not worried."

"I want to speak to them."

"Don't worry, you will."

He reached for him again, seeking his reassurance. "What happened to you? Before I got there last night? Did they hurt you?"

"I'm fine. One of them rushed me when I came home. Corman, I guess. He was strong. He knocked me out with something. He had it in a rag and put it over my nose. When I woke up, I was already tied to the chair. I knew as soon as I saw the underpants I was wearing what was happening. *Red Hills Massacre.* Your famous death scene. And just like Julian."

"They must have known, after planting the seeds of doubt in my mind at the theatre...that you would be alone."

"They could have followed you, for all we know. Seen us argue and decided that was the perfect moment."

"Oh God, Luke," he cried. "I'm so sorry. You were only involved in this because of me."

"Hey." Luke wiped the tear from his cheek. "Enough of that. The only reason they came after me, the reason Rav and Julian are dead, is because Amber and Corman are fucking psychopaths. No victim blaming. If we're blaming anyone, it's those two sick fuckers."

* * * *

The doctor came around half an hour later and gave Hudson a thorough examination. He declared he was fit to be discharged. There was no treatment for the broken coccyx other than painkillers and time. "Like a broken rib, it will get better on its own," he explained. "Sleep on your belly and take it easy for a few weeks. Try not to sit for long periods and take over-the-counter pain meds. This bone can take a long time to heal, several months, and you don't want to do anything that's going to aggravate it or set you back."

Luke had gone to Hudson's apartment to collect some clothes for his discharge, and he was alone when the police arrived. DS Coppola and DS Peters — Luke's ex-husband, Kris.

"You'd think the King was up here," Kris remarked as they entered.

"Huh?"

"Press," Benito explained. "Downstairs is swarming with them."

"Shit. I hadn't even thought of that."

"Can't blame them. It's quite the story. Local podcasters murder your understudy then come after you in a bizarre tribute to one of your movies." Benito raised his hands wide. "They're going bonkers for it."

"They murdered Rav, too," Hudson said. "I'm pretty sure it was Corman who did that, though I didn't see because of the mask."

"Don't worry, we've already checked out their apartments. We know they did it." Benito's eyes crinkled sympathetically. "Why don't you have a seat? We need to ask you a few questions and then we'll tell you what we know already."

"I'd rather stand," Hudson said, pointing to his backside.

"Oh course, sure. Sorry."

Hudson moved over to the window, steadying himself with a hand on the sill. Outside the sky was a perfect blue, clear and serene. A stark contrast to the madness of the last twelve hours. He was lost for a few seconds, before snapping himself back to the present. He took a deep breath and turned to face the detectives. "Where do you want me to start?"

He gave a thorough account of the day, from Amber and Corman trying to suggest Luke had something to do with Julian's death, to the phone call that had drawn him and Rav to the house at the coast, and the horror that unfolded from there. He was surprised by how calmly he spoke, and how much detail he was able to recall.

"One of them jumped us as soon as we arrived. Rav didn't stand a chance."

"Had you ever heard from either of them before they turned up at the rehearsal rooms?"

"Not that I'm aware of. I didn't know them or their podcast."

"It looks like we've been laying the blame for your hate mail at the wrong door," Benito said. "We don't think Robbie Wiseman sent you those letters. They were all from Amber and Corman."

He nodded numbly. It made sense. He hadn't had any interaction with Robbie for months before coming here. The stalking order had seemed to be working and had kept him away from Hudson. He assumed the recent press coverage had been too great for Robbie to resist and that's what had brought him to Blyham, rather than to deliver letters to the theatre.

"We need to go through all of their equipment, but from what we've found so far, Amber and Corman have had an unhealthy interest in you going back a long way."

"Especially that slasher film you did," Kris added. "They've got props and posters. All kind of replica masks of the killer. They were obsessed with it."

"What about Corman? How is he?"

"He'll live," Benito said. "He's awake, though he's not talking yet. Probably doesn't know what to do without his partner in crime. They were very much in it together. Not sure how well he functions alone."

"Have you found any evidence that they killed Julian?"

"There's a lot to go through, but we will. It looks like they were big on collecting souvenirs of what they did."

It was becoming too much for him to take in. "What about Luke? Amber?"

"It's not up to us. It's a decision for the prosecution service, but I can't see that it's in anyone's interest to charge him. It was self-defence. And no jury is ever going to find him guilty once the full picture is established."

He nodded, somewhat relieved. "Luke saved my life. Twice in one night. I...owe him everything."

"I know," Benito said. "I think you need to prepare yourself. Corman and Amber were obsessed with you. To the point of wanting to kill you. When we find out exactly what they were planning, you're not going to like it."

Chapter Twenty-Eight

Waiting for Resolution

One month later

Hudson sat at a shaded table in a rear corner of The Blue Pearl. He'd been avoiding public places in Blyham for the last few weeks, but today he'd found the walls of the apartment claustrophobic and oppressive. Even the balcony had felt like a prison, and he'd had to get out.

It had gone three and, after not eating all day, he'd thought that a bite to eat and a coffee would do him good. The sandwich remained untouched on his plate, though he was already on his third cup of coffee.

No one bothered him. The server had recognised him, but had kept their chat light and professional, and no one else in the bar seemed to know who he was. Amazing, considering how much coverage he'd gotten in the national press in recent weeks. Maybe the baseball cap and reading glasses were working in his favour after all. He pretended to be a character.

Someone who didn't want to be approached. He must be giving out suitable vibes.

He checked his watch again.

Luke had been at the police station for almost two hours now.

They'd said the interview would be a formality, but Hudson had insisted that Luke take a lawyer along with him anyway. What if the cops had changed their minds? Luke had said all along that the Blyham force were unpredictable. Maybe the bastards had done a U-turn and wanted to charge him with Amber's death after all.

He sighed and shifted about in his seat. His coccyx had many weeks of healing still to go, but he found that if he kept his weight forward, he could sit comfortably enough for solid periods of time. He'd been working out too and doing Pilates to aid the injury. It all seemed to be helping his recovery.

Hudson had remained in Blyham for one reason. Luke. All rational sense had told him to pack up and fly back to New York, but his heart thought differently. He couldn't leave Luke after what they'd been through, when he felt so much for him.

It was unlikely that *Darkest Blue* would ever make it to the stage. With the deaths of a producer and an actor, an injured leading man and the production mired in a murder investigation, the entire run had been cancelled. If there was any attempt to mount the play in the future, Hudson would not be part of it. He had no intention of ever going to see it. The play was cursed and had generated enough sadness and grief. It was better that it never was.

The investigation into Amber's and Corman's crimes continued. Corman had been charged with

Julian's and Rav's murders, and the attempted murders of Hudson and Luke, but the more the police dug into their computers and phones, the more they had discovered. There was a mountain of video and photographic evidence. The podcasters had been behind many of the true crime stories they had chronicled on their show, including an arson attack on a probation office and the Blyham Cat Killer. Before moving on to human murders, they'd killed a large number of pets around the city in order to have something sensational to report.

They had been working together for almost three years. Hudson was fearful of what else would be discovered since they'd met and discovered the darkness in each other.

Thanks to Luke's ex-husband's loose mouth and unprofessionalism, they'd been provided with regular updates on the police case. The attempt on Luke's life seemed to have mellowed his ex. Kris even behaved civilly towards Hudson. Maybe things were at last improving for the better in Blyham Police.

For Luke's sake, he hoped that was true.

Hudson checked his phone. He'd messaged Luke to let him know where to find him when he was done. No reply as yet.

Hudson sucked a breath through his teeth and tried to convince himself that no news could be good news.

One of the other things that had been discovered was Amber and Corman's mutual love of *Red Hills Massacre*. He failed to see how anyone could like that movie, though Luke had admitted to being a fan of it also, but if ever two twisted minds were going to bond over a film, it would have to be that piece of shit.

Hudson wouldn't have believed it possible for him to hate the film more than he already had, but he did. He'd received hundreds of requests for interviews from around the world, all wanting him to talk about the film and why it might have made him the target of the killers. He'd rejected every single one and would continue to do so for the rest of his life. Horror movies were over for him. For as long as he kept acting, he would never appear in another one.

They had their fans, and the vast majority were nice people just like Luke, but the idea had been spoiled forever.

Amber and Corman had been involved in a fucked-up, real-life remake of *Red Hills Massacre*. Courtesy of Kris, Hudson had also learnt that that they had filmed Julian's murder, taking turns to stab him while wearing the Baby Face mask. They had set up secret cameras at the theatre and filmed Hudson and Luke in his dressing room having sex. No doubt it had been intended as a titillating taster for what they had planned next.

The only solace he took from the news was that the more evidence the police uncovered, the more charges would be brought against Corman and the easier it would be to send the motherfucker to prison for the rest of his life.

Corman had made a full recovery from his head injuries and was currently on remand ahead of the court case.

Hudson looked up as the front door opened. Luke entered and glanced around.

Thank God. Hudson had had an awful feeling that Luke might also be spending the night in a police cell. He stood and waved him over, wrapping him a tight embrace as soon as he reached the table.

"I'm so relieved to see you," Hudson said, putting his hands flat against Luke's back and clinging to him. They stayed that way for a long time. "How did it go?" he said when he eventually released him.

Luke removed his light blazer and slung it over a chair, sitting down next to Hudson. Hudson took his hand and didn't let go.

"They kept me waiting ages and then they spent a long time going over everything. Understandable. I did kill someone, after all."

"You killed her in self-defence, not cold blood. There's a huge difference."

Luke nodded resolutely. He'd been putting on a brave face since that night, talking tough, but Hudson knew he'd been struggling with the reality of what he had done. Amber was a fucked-up murderer, but taking another life did not come easily to most people, whatever the circumstances. It could take Luke years to process the mental trauma of his actions. Hudson intended to be there for him and support him through every step on the path to acceptance.

"I'm in the clear," Luke said at last, looking and sounding relieved. "There will be no charges against me for killing Amber. Even her own family aren't pressing for it. A clear case of self-defence."

Hudson let out the breath he hadn't realised he'd been holding. He gripped Luke's hand tighter. "That's great news. And only right. All the evidence backs it up."

Luke managed a smile, though the tension around his eyes remained. "It doesn't mean it's over. I'll still have to testify in court against Corman. We both will."

"I know. And we'll nail the bastard. For Julian. For Rav. For what he's put their families through. For what he's done to us. We'll get him and he'll never hurt anyone again."

At last Luke's smile was genuine, though his eyes were moist. He lifted Hudson's hand to his lips and kissed. "I love you."

Hudson moved even closer and put his arms around him. "I love you, too."

* * * *

It was an afternoon a lot like the first day Hudson had visited the house on the coast. Clear, bright—a perfect summer day.

Only now the house was filled with the wrong kind of memories.

Luke had not spent another night inside the place since the attack. He'd moved into Hudson's apartment in the city and had stayed there ever since.

Luke's parents had agreed to supervise the emptying and disposal of the contents, but Luke had insisted on visiting one last time to collect any personal stuff he couldn't do without.

"You don't have to do this," Hudson said as he stepped out of the car. "Tell me where everything is, and I'll bring it out for you."

Luke shook his head, getting out. He took off his sunglasses to gaze at the house. Nothing much had changed since the last time they were here, from the exterior at least. But Luke's feelings about his former home had changed beyond recognition. The tension in his stance was obvious.

"Why don't we have a few minutes in the garden?" Hudson said, pointing to the patio furniture that stood in front of the house. Luke's parents must not have got around to selling those pieces yet.

Luke seemed relieved at the suggestion. A tight smile tugged at the corners of his mouth. "That sounds like a good idea."

Hudson took his hand as they walked across the garden. The still vibrant colours of the garden, together with the familiar scent of the sea and the warm afternoon sun, reminded Hudson of happier times. As they took a seat, the sense of relief deepened as a well-known sight bounded across the garden.

"Molly." Luke beamed as the cat ran to him. She meowed excitedly, sliding in and out of his legs, rubbing her body against his calves. He bent to stroke her head affectionately.

She purred loudly, rolling onto her back at his feet.

"She's missed you." Hudson grinned. It was great to see Luke looking so happy again.

"I've missed you too," Luke said lovingly to Molly, running his hand all along her side. She continued to meow her delight. "I hope you'll be as friendly to your next neighbours. Welcome them to the neighbourhood and keep them happy."

After a few minutes, Molly leapt onto Luke's lap and settled herself while he stroked her head.

When they finally found a permanent place to live, they'd have to get a cat of their own. Luke clearly adored animals.

Hudson gazed at the sea. Such a shame Luke's time here had ended the way it had. This place had had everything until Corman and Amber ruined it.

"I've got something to tell you," he said at last.

Luke's eyes flicked over to him. "Sounds ominous."

"It's not. At least I hope not. I've had an offer to do a TV series. A good one. It's a limited series. A comedy drama with a great pilot script."

"That's fantastic news. Especially after all the shit you've been offered."

Unbelievably, Hudson's agents had been fielding so many offers of horror films and gruesome crime shows since his name had hit the headlines again.

"I haven't said yes yet, because I wanted to run it by you first. And I didn't want to do that until you got the all-clear from the cops." He took a deep breath. Here came the crucial information. "It's going to mean filming in Canada for six months. Vancouver."

He caught the look of uncertainty that came over Luke's face and before he could reply, Hudson rushed on, "I want you to come with me. Or at least think about it. It's just six months, but the break from Blyham could be good for you. Good for us. Maybe the paper will let you take a sabbatical."

Luke let out a long breath. "Wow. I wasn't expecting that."

"And does the idea appal you?"

Now Luke gazed at him earnestly. "The exact opposite. I never thought I'd say this, but getting away from Blyham is exactly what I need right now."

Relief washed over Hudson as a broad smile spread across his face. "And it's not forever. Six months. We can come back here afterwards and see how you feel about the place then."

Luke nodded. "It's a perfect idea. I'm sure I can get the time off. Maybe even start writing that novel I've always wanted to."

Hudson leapt out of his seat and crouched beside Luke's chair, taking his hand. "You mean that? You really want to come with me? I won't take the job if you're not sure."

"I'll be pissed off if you don't take it. Of course I'll come with you. After what we've been through, I can't think of anything better than spending time together away from here."

Hudson pressed his lips to Luke's. This was all for real. They had faced the horrors of this city, and had survived. Now they had the opportunity of experiencing something new. Something positive. Something for both of them.

They were in it together, and Hudson felt certain that they always would be.

Sign up for our newsletter and find out about all our romance book releases, eBook sales and promotions, sneak peeks and FREE romance books!

Want to see more from this author?
Here's a taster for you to enjoy!

Basic Instincts:
The Dark Before Dawn
Thom Collins

Excerpt

Five songs into his first set of the evening, Jude Kalvert knew the gig was going well. The majority of the audience was paying attention to him. They listened attentively, tapping their hands and feet to the music, and mouthing along to the better-known numbers, even laughing at the banter he delivered in between. Jude had them where he wanted them.

With a small degree of confidence, he launched into one of his self-penned songs. It fit right in with the easy indie pop tunes he had delivered so far. He smiled as he strummed his guitar and sang, noticing how the bulk of the crowd continued to bob their feet as though he was playing a well-known hit.

Yes. This is what it's all about.

Jude had always enjoyed playing at The Blue Pearl. The pub had a reputation for great live music, with singers and bands performing every night and most afternoons, but it had been about seven months since his last gig here. A lot could change in that time. Thankfully, it hadn't, and his first forty-five-minute set seemed to go like the click of his fingers.

His sister Ruby was waiting when he stepped off the small stage. "That was bloody brilliant," she said, throwing her arms around him and planting an enthusiastic kiss on his cheek. "I love that new song. Are you going to record it?"

"That's the plan." He grabbed a bottle of water and guzzled greedily. His thirst seemed unquenchable.

It was quite a change of pace for Jude. He had spent the last six months working at sea on the Atlantic Star cruise ship, as part of a ten-member entertainment team. They would regularly put on four big production shows each week, full of choreography and costume changes. It was a lot of fun, but the content of the shows, especially the songs—a mix of show tunes and old time 1970s and 80s hits—were rarely to his taste. The Blue Pearl was far more his vibe, where he could play the music that meant the most to him. It still required a large repertoire of covers, but he got to perform the music of the singer-songwriters he loved, as well as a smattering of his own tunes.

Being in Blyham, his home city, made it even more special.

"Have you been writing the whole time you've been away?" Ruby asked.

"Only when time allowed." Like many people, Jude's sister believed that life on a cruise ship was one long holiday. The reality was that he hadn't had a whole day off in six months, getting just a few hours each day to himself where he could go ashore, hit the gym, or catch up on his sleep. The third option was often the most likely. He had come home with five new songs, though they all needed further development. Something he hoped to achieve in the coming weeks with his best friend and collaborator Vinnie.

"I'm so proud," Ruby said. "I wish I had a speck of your talent."

"You got the brains," he said, only half joking. Ruby had always been the really smart one between them.

"Sorry I can't stick around." She picked up her bottle of beer and drained it.

"I'm glad you came. Thanks, sis."

"Wouldn't miss it. Though someday, I want to come and see you perform on that ship."

He laughed. Ruby got queasy on the short ferry ride across the River Bly. She had no chance of keeping well on a ship bouncing through a big Atlantic Ocean swell.

"Enjoy your night," he told her. "Say hi to Craig for me."

Ruby's boyfriend was treating her to pizza, followed by a bum-numbing three-hour action movie at the local multiplex. "I'd rather stay here." She grimaced, before hugging him goodbye.

Jude slipped into the tiny dressing room at the side of the stage. It was cramped and far from comfortable, but he wanted a little peace to prepare for his next set. He had half an hour to kill. He took another bottle of water from the minibar and opened the salad box he had brought with him.

This really was a world away from his life at sea, but he appreciated being home, not having to maintain his balance on an ever-shifting stage, getting to spend time with family and friends rather than work colleagues. Jude also knew that after a few weeks at home he would start to feel the pull of ocean life again. He would miss those busy days, the cheers of a packed theatre, the salty spray of the waves, and the rocking motion of the bed lulling him to sleep.

He'd already been offered another contract, beginning in three months' time, with the chance of promotion to deputy cruise director. When the offer had been made in his last two weeks on board, he hadn't been able to consider it. All he'd wanted to do was get home and spend time with the people he loved. It was something he would have to think about in the coming weeks.

Jude was finishing his salad when there was a knock on the dressing room door. Zand Riley, the manager of The Blue Pearl, entered with a smile. "The wanderer returns," Zand said.

Jude rose to accept Zand's welcoming hug. Jude had always had a massive crush on the hot older man. Zand was probably about ten years his senior, around forty, he guessed, but he had the eagerness and enthusiasm of somebody half that age. His support for local singers and bands made him doubly attractive in Jude's eyes.

"You totally smashed that first set," Zand told him, leaning against the door frame.

"I always get a good vibe from your audiences. It makes the show so much easier."

"Different from your cruise crowds, I imagine."

"Like night and day."

"You're looking good," Zand said. "Sea air and travel obviously agrees with you."

"Thanks." He took the compliment as it was intended. Zand had a real hottie of a boyfriend and Jude knew he had no sexual interest in him. "What's been happening since I've been gone?"

"In Blyham? All the usual shit. Hate crimes, murder, homophobia, transphobia. A bunch of knuckle-dragging bigots got voted onto the city council. The first thing they did was remove the pride flag from the town hall. How's that for progress?"

"Shit. I saw bits and pieces on social media when I was away, but I tend to filter out the bad news. It just gets me down."

"There's been a lot to filter out. I shouldn't complain. We don't get the trouble in here that they've been getting up in the pink village. Julie's had their windows smashed last week. And a couple of guys were beaten up walking home from the New Inn at the weekend."

"Shit. I really thought things would have improved by now. After they caught The Strangler."

The LGBTQ+ community of Blyham had been facing issues of violence and prejudice for years. Jude realised he'd been living in his cruise ship bubble where bigotry and intolerance were not accepted. On his last voyage, two passengers had been thrown off the ship for using racist slurs against members of the bar team.

"Some things have gotten better, a little, I guess, but not enough to notice. Take care when you're about, is what I'm saying. It's not safe to walk around on your own. Hell, it's not really that safe if you're with somebody else."

Jude sighed and wanted to change the subject. It was depressing and he had to get himself in a good headspace for his second set. "I saw the poster for the acts you've got booked this month. It all looks pretty cool. I'm going to check some of them out when I'm not working." There had been a vast array of musical talent on board the ship, but they were all of a type. Solid middle of the road stuff. Jude was dying to hear a more diverse range of music.

Zand nodded. He had always been a champion of local talent. "Yeah, we've got some really good acts coming up." He pulled out his phone. "I don't suppose you're free a week on Sunday? My afternoon booking has cancelled on me."

Jude didn't have to consult his own calendar. He'd only been home a few days and hadn't managed to secure more than a handful of gigs. He was doing a show at a café bar near Durham that same evening but could easily find time for a laid-back matinee the same day. "I'll do it."

"Perfect. Just keep it low key and acoustic. That's what the Sunday afternoon crowd come in for."

"Whatever you want." The Blue Pearl was his favourite venue in the whole city. Jude was even more delighted when Zand booked him for another evening show the following month.

On his time off from the ship, he planned to work hard to secure as many gigs as possible to build up his reputation and develop his songwriting skills. He'd been lucky enough to make his living from music these last few years, and he was not about to slow down.

When Zand left, he prepared himself for the second show, mussing up his hair and putting on a fresh spritz of aftershave. He took a handful of selfies and deleted all but his favourite ones. That was another job on his to do list — to build up his social media following in the next two months. He was not a fan of posting photos or videos of himself, but it was a necessary part of the job these days. It was a not matter of wanting to do it or not. He *had* to do it.

He had managed to compile a pretty extensive show reel of his performances on the ship, and now he wanted to do the same for his solo gigs.

If people can't find you online, you don't really exist. It was not a mantra he completely believed, but he repeated it enough to force himself into making the content.

The bar had filled up a lot during his break. All the tables were occupied, and there was a large pack of people standing around. Alcohol flowed, and so did the conversation. This would be a tougher crowd to command. Undeterred, he stepped onto the stage with his guitar. Jude loved a challenge.

The later show was more upbeat, more raucous and, after covers by The Killers and Sam Fender, he noticed people had started paying attention to him. Pretty soon the room was wild, and they applauded eagerly at the end of every song. Sweat dripped into his eyes and ran down his cheeks as he tore through the setlist and thrummed his guitar. There was nothing better than this.

After two encores, he was absolutely elated. His head buzzed with the excitement. He told the audience when they could catch him playing again and where to find his music online. That was another job on his growing list of things to achieve. He already had one EP of original songs on the streaming services. Before going back to sea—if he went back to sea—he wanted to record and release another. He had a good idea of what the songs would be but was open to creating something new before going into the recording studio.

Zand came over as he was unplugging his gear and patted him on the shoulder. Through it was a purely platonic gesture, it sent a frisson of electricity through him. Jude realised he hadn't had sex in weeks. The last time had been an unsatisfactory fumble with a crew member from the Shore Destinations team.

Suddenly he was very horny.

But he couldn't get any ideas about Zand. This hottie was strictly off limits.

"You were brilliant. Absolutely brilliant," Zand said. "I think you're even better now than the last time you were here. Whatever you've been learning on that ship, it's working."

Jude grinned widely. He'd already been charged from the energy of the audience. Zand's compliments made him feel even better. "It means a lot to hear that. Thanks for saying it."

Jude had heard a lot of bad things about Blyham of late, including from Zand tonight, but from his point of view this evening, there was no better place to be.

He was so glad to be back.

* * * *

It took a while for Jude to get his equipment packed up at the end of the night. So many people wanted to come over and talk to him.

"I remember seeing you play here a few years ago," one woman told him. She was slightly tipsy and shouting, waving her gin glass with enthusiasm. "I'm so glad you've returned."

"So am I," he answered her. "I hope to be here a lot more if possible."

The DJ was impatient to set up her own gear. Jude mouthed an apology and hurriedly put his stuff away. The live music had come to an end, but the bar stayed open until two, with the DJ playing all the way. Earlier in the evening, he'd considered staying behind for a while, but by the end of his last set, he was starving. The salad he'd had in the break had barely satisfied, and he was desperate for something more substantial.

His car was parked in the alley behind the bar, and it took two trips to carry everything out. It was a surprisingly mild night for late September. He left his jacket in the car when he went back inside to thank Zand and say goodnight.

The DJ already had the crowd going and the small dance floor was packed.

"Thanks again," he said, patting Zand on his well-muscled shoulder. "I had a great time up there."

"So did everyone else, Jude. I've had loads of people come up already to say they want to see you again. Maybe you've been wasted on that fancy ship."

Jude laughed, though he was deeply flattered. "I'll see you a week on Sunday then. Bye for now."

His stomach rumbled as he walked back to the car. There used to be a fantastic all-night café up on the edge of the pink quarter that did the best pizzas he'd had outside of Italy. He hadn't had a chance to check it out since he got back, but he hoped it was still there. Small businesses in Blyham had taken a massive hit in recent years and whenever he returned, it seemed like another two or three had closed.

The only way to find out was to get his arse up there.

Jude slipped behind the wheel and turned on the engine. As the headlights came on, they illuminated two men locked in a passionate embrace in the doorway of the building opposite. One of the men had his back to Jude and his jeans shoved to mid-thigh, exposing his nice, chunky butt cheeks. They were flawless white in the glare of the lights.

Startled, they broke their kiss and turned towards the car. Shock was written large on both of their faces as they shielded their eyes against the glare. One of the men was a fair bit taller than the other. The shorter man bent to grab his jeans, hitching them over his fine arse, while the other hurried to shove a hard-on into his pants.

They were both incredibly sexy and Jude felt awful for interrupting their fun.

He wound down the windows. "Sorry, guys," he shouted. "I'm leaving. Don't mind me. Keep doing what you're doing and have a brilliant night."

He put the car in gear. As the headlights swung around, he saw the two men smile. The short guy with the great bum gave him a wave.

Damn. That unexpected peep show had only made Jude hornier. He adjusted the rapid hardness in his own jeans.

He had an itch that needed a scratch. Jude realised he had to get laid, and soon.

It was one more thing to put on his to-do list.

About the Author

Thom Collins is the author of the *Jagged Shores* and *Basic Instincts* series, the *Anthem Trilogy* and *Closer by Morning*. He has lived in the North East of England his whole life. He grew up in Northumberland and now lives in County Durham with his husband and cat. He loves all kinds of genre fiction, especially thrillers, romance and horror. He is also a cookery book addict with far too many titles cluttering his shelves. When not writing he can be found in the kitchen trying out new recipes. He's a keen traveler but with a dislike of flying that gets worse with age. Since 2013 he prefers to see the world by sea.

Thom loves to hear from readers. You can find his contact information, website details and author profile page at https://www.firstforromance.com

ENTWINED PUBLISHING

www.ingramcontent.com/pod-product-compliance
Lightning Source LLC
Chambersburg PA
CBHW020818260626
47169CB00003B/730